Caddie Woodlawn

CAROL RYRIE BRINK

Aladdin Paperbacks
NEW YORK   LONDON   TORONTO   SYDNEY

To Gram
whose tales of her childhood in Wisconsin
gave a lonely little girl many happy hours

ALADDIN PAPERBACKS
An imprint of Simon & Schuster Children's Publishing Division
1230 Avenue of the Americas, New York, NY 10020
Text copyright 1935 by Macmillan Publishing Company
Text copyright renewed 1963 by Carol Ryrie Brink
Illustrations copyright © 1973 by Simon & Schuster, Inc.
All rights reserved, including the right of reproduction in whole or in part in any form.
ALADDIN PAPERBACKS and colophon are trademarks of Simon & Schuster, Inc.
Also available in a Simon & Schuster Books for Young Readers hardcover edition.
Manufactured in the United States of America
First Aladdin Paperbacks edition 1990
This Aladdin Paperbacks edition December 2006
10 9 8 7 6 5 4 3 2
Library of Congress Cataloging-in-Publication Data
Brink, Carol Ryrie, 1895–1981
Caddie Woodlawn / Carol Ryrie Brink; illustrated by Trina Schart Hyman.
p. cm.
Reprint. Originally published: New York: Macmillian, 1935.
Summary: The adventures of an eleven-year-old tomboy growing up on the Wisconsin frontier in the mid-nineteenth century.
ISBN-13: 978-0-02-713670-8 (hc)
ISBN-10: 0-02-713670-1 (hc)
[I. Frontier and pioneer life—Wisconsin—Fiction.] I. Hyman, Trina Schart, ill. II. Title.
PZ7.B78Cad 1990
[Fic]—dc20 89-18357 CIP AC
ISBN-13: 978-1-4169-4028-9 (pbk)
ISBN-10: 1-4169-4028-6 (pbk)

Author's Note

Twelve miles south of Menomonie, Wisconsin, there is a pretty wayside park named in honor of Caddie Woodlawn. In it you may picnic or rest or enter a small gray house and see exactly where Caddie and Tom and Warren once lived. You may follow a trail out to Chimney Bluffs or go to the river where the Little Steamer used to dock in the days when the river was higher and when Dunnville was a promising town. Now the town has almost disappeared. While Caddie and Tom and Warren were living there, they would have been much surprised to learn that a hundred years later thousands of visitors from thirty-seven states and six foreign countries would sign the guest book in the Caddie Woodlawn house in one year. They would not have believed a word of it.

Caddie Woodlawn was my grandmother. Her real name was Caddie Woodhouse. All of the names in the book, except one, are changed a little bit. The names are partly true, partly made up, just as the facts of the book are mainly true but have sometimes been slightly changed to make them fit better into the story. The one name that remains unchanged is that of Robert Ireton. I liked the name and I thought that, since hired men often moved from place to place for seasonal work, no one was likely to remember him. But even Robert is remembered today in this part of Wisconsin, and you may go to visit his grave.

There was a strong bond of love between my grandmother and me. As soon as I could walk I used to run away to see her. She was fun to be with and she always had something interesting to tell me. By the time I was eight I had lost both of my parents, and I went to live with my grandmother and an unmarried aunt. I had no brothers or sisters. Gram and Aunt and I were the family, and we lived in northern Idaho in an old-fashioned house on a big town lot. It was almost like a tiny farm with a barn for my pony and room for dogs, cats, chickens and canary birds. There were many different kinds of fruit trees, and in cherry season I used to climb up to a comfortable branch and sit reading a book and eating cherries. I was happy, but I was often lonely and I learned to amuse myself by reading, drawing, writing, and telling myself long, continued stories. The storytelling came naturally, because Gram and Aunt had told me so many stories that I thought I knew just how the best ones ought to go. I particularly loved to hear about Gram's pioneer childhood in Wisconsin. Being an only child made me want especially to hear about her many brothers and sisters who lived together in such good nature and love. The only one of them that I ever saw was Hetty. I knew her as Great-aunt Ett, and I used to look forward to her visits with us. Then the stories flew thick and fast, and I sat spellbound, listening, listening!

It was many years later that I remembered these stories of Caddie's childhood, and I said to myself, "If I loved them so much, perhaps other children would like them, too." Caddie was still alive while I was writing, and I sent many letters to her, asking about the details that I did not remember clearly. She was pleased when the book was done. "There is only one thing that I do not understand," she said. "You never knew my mother and father and my brothers—how could you write about them exactly as they were?"

"But, Gram," I said, "you told me."

After the book was published, schoolchildren used to come to see her on her birthday and sing for her or give her little presents. This pleased her very much. She lived to be almost eighty-six years of age. Like a true pioneer she had come all across the country from Boston to Wisconsin to Idaho to the Pacific Ocean. She had many troubles in her life, but she always looked out cheerfully at the world and found it a good place. She noticed people and the interesting things that happened to them, and she found these things worth retelling.

For myself and two younger cousins, Gram represented kindness and good sense, justice tempered by humor, and love and security. After her death we had a line from the Bible carved on her gravestone: "Her candle goeth not out by night."

CAROL RYRIE BRINK

February 6, 1973

Contents

1 · *Three Adventurers*

In 1864 Caddie Woodlawn was eleven, and as wild a little tomboy as ever ran the woods of western Wisconsin. She was the despair of her mother and of her elder sister, Clara. But her father watched her with a little shine of pride in his eyes, and her brothers accepted her as one of themselves without a question. Indeed, Tom, who was two years older, and Warren, who was two years younger than Caddie, needed Caddie to link them together into an inseparable trio. Together they got in and out of more scrapes and adventures than any one of them could have imagined alone. And in those pioneer days, Wisconsin offered plenty of opportunities for adventure to three wide-eyed, red-headed youngsters.

On a bright Saturday afternoon in the early fall, Tom and Caddie and Warren Woodlawn sat on a bank of the Menomonie River, or Red Cedar as they call it now, taking off their clothes. Their red heads shone in the sunlight. Tom's hair was the darkest, Caddie's the nearest golden, and nine-year-old Warren's was plain carrot color. Not one of the three knew how to swim, but they were going across the river nevertheless. A thin thread of smoke beyond the bend on the other side of the river told them that the Indians were at work on a birch-bark canoe.

"Do you think the Indians around here would ever get mad and massacre folks like they did up north?" wondered Warren, tying his shirt up in a little bundle.

"No, sir," said Tom, "not these Indians!"

"Not Indian John, anyhow," said Caddie. She had just unfastened the many troublesome little buttons on the back of her tight-waisted dress, and, before taking it off, she paused a moment to see if she could balance a fresh-water clam shell on her big toe. She found that she could.

"No, not Indian John!" she repeated decidedly, having got the matter of the clam shell off her mind. "Even if he does have a scalp belt," she added. The thought

of the scalp belt always made her hair prickle delightfully up where her scalp lock grew.

"Naw," said Tom, "the fellows who spread those massacree stories are just big-mouthed scared-cats who
don't know the Indians, I guess."

"Big-mouthed scared cats," repeated Warren, admiring Tom's command of language.

"Big-mouthed scared-cats," echoed a piping voice
from the bank above. Seven-year-old Hetty, who flut-
tered wistfully on the outer edge of their adventures,
filed away Tom's remark in her active brain. It would
be useful to tell to Mother, some time when Mother
was complaining about Tom's language. The three
below her paid no attention to Hetty's intrusion. Their
red heads, shining in the sunlight, did not even turn in
her direction. Hetty's hair was red, too, like Father's,
but somehow, in spite of her hair, she belonged on the
dark-haired side of the family where Mother and
Clara and all the safe and tidy virtues were. She
poised irresolutely on the bank above the three adven-
turous ones. If they had only turned around and
looked at her! But they were enough in themselves.
She could not make up her mind what to do. She
wanted to go with them, and yet she wanted just as
much to run home and tell Mother and Clara what
they were about to do. Hetty was the self-appointed

newsbearer of the family. Wild horses could not pre-
vent her from being the first to tell, whatever it was
that happened.

Tom and Caddie and Warren finished undressing,
tied their clothes into tight bundles, and stepped out
into the river. The water was low after a long, hot summer, but still it looked cold and deep. Hetty shud-
dered. She had started to undo one shoe, but now she
quickly tied it up again. She had made up her mind.
She turned around and flew across the fields to tell
Mother.

Tom knew from experience that he could just keep
his chin above water and touch bottom with his toes
across the deep part of the river. It would have been
over Caddie's and Warren's heads, but, if they held
onto Tom and kept their feet paddling, they could just
keep their heads above water. They had done it before. Tom went first with his bundle of clothes balanced on his head. Caddie came next, clutching Tom's
shoulder with one hand and holding her bundle of
clothes on top of her head with the other. Warren
clung to Caddie's shoulder in the same manner, bal-
ancing his own clothes with his free hand. They
moved slowly and carefully. If Tom lost his footing or
fell, they would all go down together and be swept
away by the current toward the village below. But the

other two had every confidence in Tom, and Tom had not the slightest reason to doubt himself. They looked like three beavers, moving silently across the current —three heads with three bundles and a little wake of ripples trailing out behind them. Last of all came Nero, the farm dog, paddling faithfully behind them. But Hetty was already out of sight.

Presently there was solid riverbed beneath their feet again. The three children scrambled out on the other side, shook themselves as Nero did, and pulled on their dry, wrinkled clothing.

"Hurry up, Caddie," called Tom. "You're always the last to dress."

"So would you be, too, Tom, if you had so many buttons!" protested Caddie. She came out of the bushes struggling with the back of her blue denim dress. Relenting, Tom turned his superior intelligence to the mean task of buttoning her up the back.

"I wish Mother'd let me wear boys' clothes," she complained.

"Huh!" said Warren. "She thinks you're tomboy enough already."

"But they're so much quicker," said Caddie regretfully.

Now that they were dressed, they sped along the river bank in the direction of the smoke. Several Indian canoes were drawn up on shore in the shelter of a little cove and beyond them in a clearing the Indians moved to and fro about a fire. Propped on two logs was the crude framework of a canoe which was already partly covered with birch bark. The smell of birch smoke and hot pitch filled the air. Caddie lifted her head and sniffed. It was perfume to her, as sweet as the perfume of the clover fields. Nero sniffed, too, and growled low in his throat.

The three children stopped at the edge of the clearing and watched. Even friendly Indians commanded fear and respect in those days. A lean dog, with a wolfish look, came forward barking.

He and Nero circled about each other, little ridges of bristling hair along their spines, their tails wagging suspiciously. Suddenly the Indian dog left Nero and came toward Caddie.

"Look!" said Caddie. "It's Indian John's dog." The dog's tail began to wag in a friendlier manner, and Caddie reached out and patted his head.

By this time the Indians had noticed the children. They spoke among themselves and pointed. Some of them left their work and came forward.

In all the seven years since the Woodlawns had come from Boston to live in the big house on the prairie, the Indians had never got used to seeing them. White men and their children they had seen often enough, but never such as these, who wore, above their pale faces, hair the color of flame and sunset. During the first year the children spent in Wisconsin, the Indians had come from all the country around to look at them. They had come in groups, crowding into Mrs. Woodlawn's kitchen in their silent moccasins, touching the children's hair and staring. Poor Mrs. Woodlawn, frightened nearly out of her wits, had fed them bread or beans or whatever she had on hand, and they had gone away satisfied.

"Johnny, my dear," Mrs. Woodlawn had complained to her husband, "those frightful savages will eat us out of house and home."

"Patience, Harriet," said her husband, "we have enough and to spare."

"But, Johnny, the way they look at the children's hair frightens me. They might want a red scalp to hang to their belts."

Caddie remembered very vividly the day, three years before, when she had gone unsuspecting into the store in the village. As she went in the door, a big Indian had seized her and held her up in the air while he took a leisurely look at her hair. She had been so frightened that she had not even cried out, but hung there, wriggling in the Indian's firm grasp, and gazing desperately about the store for help.

The storekeeper had laughed at her, saying in a

reassuring voice: "You needn't be afraid, Caddie. He's a good Indian. It's Indian John."

That was the strange beginning of a friendship, for a kind of friendship it was, that had grown up between Caddie and Indian John. The boys liked Indian John, too, but it was at Caddie and her red-gold curls that the big Indian looked when he came to the farm, and it was for Caddie that he left bits of oddly carved wood and once a doll—such a funny doll with a tiny head made of a pebble covered with calico, black horsehair braids, calico arms and legs, and a buckskin dress! John's dog knew his master's friends. Caddie had been kind to him and he accepted her as a friend.

He rubbed his head against her now as she patted his rough hair. Indian John left his work on the canoe and came forward.

"You like him dog?" he said, grinning. He was flattered when anyone patted his dog.

"Yes," said Caddie, "he's a good dog."

"Will you let us see how you put the canoe together?" asked Tom eagerly.

"You come look," said the Indian.

They followed him to the half-finished canoe. Grunting and grinning, the Indians took up their work. They fastened the pliable sheaths of birch bark into place on the light framework, first sewing them together with buckskin thongs, then cementing them with the hot pitch. The children were fascinated. Their own canoe on the lake was an Indian canoe. But it had been hollowed out of a single log. They had seen the birch-bark canoes on the river, but had never been so close to the making of one. They were so intent on every detail that time slipped by unheeded. Even the squaws, who came up behind them to examine their hair, did not take their attention from the building of the canoe. Caddie shook her head impatiently, flicking her curls out of their curious fingers, and went on watching.

But after a while Warren said: "Golly! I'm hungry." Perhaps it was the odor of jerked venison, simmering over the fire, which had begun to mingle with the odors of birch and pitch, that made Warren remember he was hungry.

"You're always hungry," said Tom, the lofty one, in a tone of disgust.

"Well, I am, too," said Caddie positively, and that settled it. The sun was beginning to swing low in the sky, and, once they had made up their minds, they were off at once. As quickly as they had come, they returned along the river bank to their crossing place. The Indians stared after them. They did not understand these curious red and white children of the white man, nor how they went and came.

Soon three bundles, three dirty faces, and three fiery heads, shining in the red autumn sun, crossed the river with a little trail of ripples behind them. Safe on the other bank, the three hastily pulled on their clothes and started to take a short cut through the woods, Nero trotting at their heels.

"Hetty probably told Mother, and Mother may be mad at us for going across the river without asking her," said Tom, beginning to turn his thoughts toward home.

"She never said we couldn't," protested Warren.

"Well, maybe she hadn't thought of such a good way of getting across," said Tom, doubtfully.

"Look!" said Caddie. She had stopped beside some hazel brush and was gazing at it with clasped hands. "Nuts! They're ready to pick."

"They're green," said Warren.

"No, they're just right to pick now, if we spread them on the woodshed roof to dry," said Tom judicially. "But we haven't much time." He began to fill his pockets. The others followed his example—only Caddie, who had no pockets, caught up the edges of her skirt and made a bag of that. The boys' pockets were soon filled.

"Come on," said Tom, "we've got enough." But Caddie's skirt was not half filled, and she didn't want to

go. Warren was thinking of supper and Tom was remembering that he was the eldest of the three, and
that the longer they were gone, the more time his
mother would have in which to get angry.

"All right for you," he said, "I'm going home and
you'd better come, too." Crackling and rustling
through the dry leaves and underbrush, the boys went
home. Tom whistled to Nero, but Nero pretended not
to hear, for Caddie was his favorite.

Caddie picked furiously, filling her skirt. It was not
often that she got more nuts than Tom. Today she
would have more than anybody. An evening stillness
crept through the golden woods. Suddenly Caddie
knew that she had better go or supper would be begun. To be late for a meal was one of the unpardon-
able sins in the Woodlawn family. Clutching the edges
of her heavy skirt, she began to run. A thorn reached
out and tore her sleeve, twigs caught in her tangled
hair, her face was dirty and streaked with perspira-
tion, but she didn't stop running until she reached the
farmhouse. In fact, she didn't stop even then, for the
deserted look of the yard told her that they were all at
supper. She rushed on, red and disheveled, and flung
open the dining-room door.

There she stopped for the first time, frozen with
astonishment and dismay. It wasn't an ordinary sup-

per. It was a company supper! Everybody was calm and clean and sedate, and at one end of the table sat the circuit rider! Paralyzed with horror, Caddie's fingers let go her shirt, and a flood of green hazelnuts rolled all over the floor. In a terrible lull in the conversation they could be heard bumping and rattling to the farthest corners of the room.

2 · The Circuit Rider

"How do you do, Caroline Augusta?" said the circuit rider in his deep voice—that voice which filled the schoolhouse with the fervor of his praying. The circuit rider was the only person who bothered to remember that Caddie was really Caroline Augusta and that Hetty was Henrietta. He turned his dark, deep-set eyes on Mrs. Woodlawn, who sat beside him at the end of the long table.

"When are you going to begin making a young lady out of this wild Indian, Mrs. Woodlawn?" he inquired.

The cameo brooch, which she wore only on Sundays or special occasions, rose and fell on Mrs. Woodlawn's bosom. The cameo earrings trembled in her ears, but she answered in as calm a voice as she could muster.

"You must ask my husband that question, Mr. Tanner."

"Caddie!" said Mr. Woodlawn abruptly. "Don't stand there staring, my child. Get washed and to table." Caddie disappeared in an instant. But, as she went, she heard her father saying: "Yes, Mr. Tanner, it is my fault that Caddie is running wild instead of making samplers and dipping candles. I will tell you why."

Caddie heard no more, but she knew what Father had to say. She loved to hear him say it in his deep, quiet voice. He would be telling how frail she and little Mary had been when they came to Wisconsin from Boston, and how, after little Mary had died, he had begged his wife to let him try an experiment with Caddie. "Harriet," he had said, "I want you to let Caddie run wild with the boys. Don't keep her in the house learning to be a lady. I would rather see her learn to plow than make samplers, if she can get her health by doing so. I believe it is worth trying. Bring the other girls up as you like, but let me have Caddie."

So, for seven years, Caddie had run the woods with Tom and Warren. She was no longer pale or delicate. She was brown and strong, and, if Tom climbed a tree, Caddie climbed a taller one. If Warren caught a snake, Caddie went after a longer one. Her mother and sisters looked at her and sighed, but Father smiled and knew that he had been a good doctor.

As these things went through her mind, Caddie ran a comb through her tangled curls and splashed water over her red, dusty face. A few moments later, when she slipped silently into her place between Tom and Warren, the grownups were talking of something else and no one paid any attention to her.

Tom and Warren, still a little untidy and flushed from the afternoon's escapade, glanced at her mischievously. They had come through the barn and seen the circuit rider's horse munching oats in the extra stall. Hastily they had cleaned themselves at the pump and got to the supper table in the very nick of time. Across the table Clara, Hetty, and little Minnie, in white aprons and neat braids, sat up straight and clean with their eyes fixed piously on the circuit rider's face. Even baby Joe, in his high chair, trying his new tooth on a silver spoon, was in spotless white. Mrs. Conroy, the hired girl, moved about the table with fresh supplies of food. Her eyes rested on Caddie in silent amusement. Caddie was her favorite among the Woodlawn children, largely because of the amusing scrapes the child got herself into. Mr. Woodlawn sent a heaping plate of beans and brown bread down to his second daughter, and Caddie ate obediently. But she was smarting with disgrace. Beneath the table, she could still feel some of her hazelnuts rolling about under her feet. And the circuit rider had asked Mother when she intended making a young lady out of her! A young lady, indeed! Who wanted to be a young lady? Certainly not Caddie! But still there were times when it was uncomfortable *not* to be one, even with Father's loyal support.

They were talking about the Indian massacres now, and, forgetting herself, Caddie began to listen. Nowadays everyone talked of the Civil War, which seemed far away from Wisconsin, and of the Indian massacres which seemed uncomfortably near.

"It's those Southerners who come North and incite the Indians to rebellion, just to make more trouble for the North," said Mrs. Woodlawn decidedly.

"Yes," said Mr. Tanner, "I fear that we cannot trust the Indians, even when they seem to be friendly."

"I don't believe we'll have massacres here, Mr. Tanner," said Father. "I do trust these Indians."

"It's true enough that they ought to be loyal to us," cried Mrs. Woodlawn, smiling at her husband. "Goodness knows, I've fed them enough victuals, and, of course, you know how my husband has treated them?"

"Someone told me that you had remodeled the guns

of the whole tribe, Woodlawn. Is that possible?" asked the circuit rider.

Mr. Woodlawn laughed. "Well," he said, "that's about the size of it, although that wasn't my intention when I started it. As a compliment to the chief of the tribe, when I came here to install the mill, I replaced the old flintlock on his gun with a spring lock. The old fellow was delighted. I thought that that was the end of the affair, but the next day when I went to the mill, there was the chief waiting for me with his whole tribe. And every man of them had brought his flint-lock gun to have a spring lock put on it. It kept me busy for a week, but the mill company was glad to pay for the locks to insure the Indians' friendship. We've never regretted it, and I don't think we shall have cause to later."

The children loved this familiar story and were sorry when the conversation drifted on to other things. But, when Mr. Tanner began to recount his travels and adventures since the last night he had spent under their roof, they were once more enthralled.

In those days the circuit riders, or traveling ministers, served large territories, riding from place to place and holding services in cabins or schoolhouses. Mr. Tanner was one of these. Weathered by sun and rain and snow, he rode from day to day over a parish which covered most of western Wisconsin. Weddings and christenings were put off until his arrival, and sometimes he found new-made graves awaiting his benediction. The settlers always opened their homes to him, and it was a great occasion when they could entertain the circuit rider. Everyone stood in awe of him. He was not only a man of God who could wrestle in spiritual battle with angels and spirits of evil, but it was said that there was not a man on his circuit who could show a strength of muscle equal to his. When, in his deep voice, he spoke of punishment for sinners, the little schoolhouse seemed to be filled with the crackling roar of the fires of hell.

But, when he sat with the Woodlawns at their table, all his sternness fell away. It was perhaps the only place on his circuit where he felt entirely at home. Their home, the largest in the neighborhood, was the one expected to offer him hospitality. But there was another reason why he always stayed there. Mr. Tanner was from Boston, too. He loved the beans and brown bread on Saturday night and the familiar talk of home. For him, as for Mrs. Woodlawn, the real beauty and meaning of life centered in the churches, the bookshops, the lecture rooms of Boston. They shared their bits of news and gossip and recalled old scenes and events as homesick people love to do. Mr. Woodlawn heard them with quiet amusement. He was entirely happy on the outskirts of civilization. Here he could breathe freely as he had never done in the narrow streets of Boston. His own home had been in England, but he did not speak of the past. The children, all except Clara, who remembered and loved Boston, listened with wide eyes of astonishment. For how could anyone prefer Boston to this enchanting place of adventure, of lake and river, prairie and forest?

When the meal was finished, the circuit rider rose and went to his saddlebags which he had left on the back porch. He dusted them carelessly and opened one. He took out first his well-worn Bible for the family prayers which were never forgotten when Mr. Tanner spent the night. Then he took out something else which suddenly made Caddie's eyes sparkle with interest. She forgot her embarrassment and came to stand beside him. It was a small clock.

"Woodlawn," said the minister, "I've brought you something to repair for me. There is not a soul on the circuit who knows how to tinker a clock as you do."

Mr. Woodlawn smiled. His workshop was already full of clocks which people had brought to him from miles around. When there was time from his farm and his duties as master mechanic at the mill, he took the neighbors' clocks apart and oiled, mended, or refitted parts to them. He was the only man in that part of the country who could do it, and, although he liked the work well enough, it was sometimes irksome to have so much of it to do. But Caddie never tired of seeing new clocks come in. She liked to see them wag their pendulums and hear their busy ticking. Her eager fingers itched to help her father take them apart and set them in motion once again.

"What's wrong with it?" she asked.

The circuit rider hesitated. He knew all about horses and ways of predicting the weather; he could quote you almost any passage in the Bible and make clear the book of Revelations. But anything with wheels or cogs or springs was an unfathomable mystery to him.

"Well," he said, "I don't rightly know. I was winding it up one night, when suddenly it gave a little gasp and a long sigh, like a soul departing from the body; and it wouldn't go after that. Sometimes, from force of habit, I take it out at night and start to wind it. Then I miss its genial tick, and I feel as if I am looking at the face of a dead friend."

A dead friend! The phrase sank into Caddie's mind. Perhaps that was why she always hated to see an unwound clock standing idle.

Mrs. Woodlawn had come to join the group. "Jacob

Allen, Tremont St., Boston," she read from the back of the clock. "Think of that! How many times I have been in and out of Jacob Allen's shop! Dear! Dear!"

"Yes," said Mr. Tanner, "it is a friend from home."

"I'll mend it for you tonight," said Mr. Woodlawn.

"No! No!" cried Mr. Tanner hastily. "Saturday's sun has gone down. I like to think that the Sabbath has begun. No, I would rather talk with you tonight, my friend. I'll leave my clock until I come back again. It may be two or three months this time. I'm going back into the interior to a new settlement where no one has yet brought the word of God."

Caddie slipped away to join Tom and Warren on the back step. They sat together, and Nero lay close to their feet. Out by the barn, Robert Ireton was strumming his banjo and singing softly. Of the three hired men, he was the one the children all loved best. It was Robert Ireton who had taught them most of the songs they knew. They knew the song he was singing now. It tickled their ears but did not lure them farther than the step. Behind the barn there were northern lights, long white fingers shooting up in the blackness of the sky; and the three adventurers were overcome by that delicious weariness which suddenly overtakes one at the end of an outdoor day.

"Golly! Tomorrow—no, Monday," said Tom, "I'm going to make a canoe like that one the Indians were making—a little one, with birch bark and pitch." But Caddie and Warren did not bother to answer.

Presently their mother came to the door and called them in to family prayers. They were a little stiff and unaccustomed to their knees, for they were used to saying their prayers in bed. Everyone was there. Even Robert Ireton came in, too, looking uneasy and strange with neither a pitchfork nor a banjo in his hands. The yellow lamplight slanted across the bowed heads. Only half listening to the words, Caddie felt herself being lifted and borne along by the circuit rider's voice. It was a kind of music—different from the twanging of the banjo or the birds at dawn, more like the falling of water over the mill wheel or the chanting of the Indians. It aroused and stirred her. There was a silence after the deep "Amen." And then the silence was broken by a gentle snore. Warren had gone to sleep with his head bent devoutly on the back of a chair. Caddie shook him hastily and the children trooped up to bed.

Caddie, Hetty, and little Minnie shared the same room. Caddie helped the younger ones with their difficult buttons and tumbled them into their beds. Then she sat a long time, drawing off her own clothes slowly and straining her ears to hear the conversation which went on below. Her father and Mr. Tanner were talking about the war, with an occasional word from her mother. The Civil War seemed remote to the children of western Wisconsin; and yet Father had paid a man to fight in his place, and Tom Hill, one of the hired men, had gone away to fight in it, and, when visitors came to the farm, the grownups always sat late into the night discussing it. Once Caddie had seen President Lincoln—he was Mr. Lincoln then. She had been quite a little girl and they had taken her to St. Louis for a visit. There had been a torchlight procession and someone had held her up to watch it from a window. And Mr. Lincoln had been in the procession. She had never forgotten the deep-lined face of the great man. Caddie slipped on her nightgown and crept to the open window where she could hear the voices from below more clearly.

"If it weren't for my wife and children," her father was saying, "Englishman and peace lover though I am, I should be out there fighting for abolition."

"That's not the usual English sentiment, Woodlawn," said Mr. Tanner. "The English aristocrats see no wrong in slavery."

When he answered, her father's gentle voice was suddenly bitter. "Ah, the English aristocrats!" he cried. "I am proud to say that I do not see things from the aristocratic point of view."

"Johnny!" cried her mother reproachfully, almost warningly, it seemed. His voice fell to a lower key, but it was still vibrant with emotion.

"God created all men free and equal," he said, "and men themselves must come to understand that truth at last!"

Shivering in the chill night air of autumn, Caddie went to bed. She crept in with Hetty, who had made a warm nest for herself and was peacefully asleep. Sometimes Caddie envied Mother and Clara, who were so dark and calm and beautiful, who seemed to find it so easy to be clean and good. But tonight her father's words echoed in her ears. She did not quite understand them, nor know why Father was so bitter when he spoke of England. She only knew that whatever Father said was true, and that she loved him better than anybody else on earth. She was glad that her hair was rough and red like his.

3 · *Pigeons in the Sky*

The next day was Sunday, and, of course, the school-house was opened and everyone went to church. Mrs. Woodlawn brought a bunch of her autumn flowers to decorate the desk. She had driven over early with her husband and Mr. Tanner to open and air the school-house which had been closed since summer. The children followed on foot. They had a mile to go, across a field and along a dusty road. They rubbed their feet through the tall grass by the schoolhouse gate to take the dust off their Sunday shoes. People from all the surrounding farms and homesteads had come to hear the circuit rider speak. Even Sam Hankinson was there, sitting in a back seat with his three little half-breed children about his knees. But his Indian wife stayed outside. Caddie peeped at them curiously through her fingers when Mr. Tanner's prayer grew very long. How would it be to have an Indian for a mother, she wondered? Then she looked at Mrs. Woodlawn, so fine in her full black silk with the cameo brooch and earrings and the small black hat, and she was glad that this was Mother. And yet, she thought, she would not be ashamed of an Indian mother, as Sam Hankinson seemed to be ashamed of his Indian wife.

The next day the circuit rider rode away on his horse. Father set his clock upon the shelf to be mended later, and life went on again as usual. But now the children began to talk about when Uncle Edmund would come, for Uncle Edmund always came with the pigeons in the fall. He made his annual visit when the shooting was at its best, for he was an eager if not a very skillful sportsman.

Mrs. Woodlawn sighed. "No one can say that I am not a devoted sister," she said, "but the prospect of a visit from Edmund always fills me with alarm. My house is turned upside down, my children behave like wild things, there is nothing but noise and confusion."

"But Ma—" cried Tom.

"Don't Ma me, my child," said Mrs. Woodlawn calmly.

"But, Mother," persisted Tom, defending his hero. "Uncle Edmund knows the most tricks——"

"And jokes!" cried Caddie.

"Remember when he put the hairbrush in Caddie's bed?" shouted Warren.

"And the time he put a frog in a covered dish on the supper table, and when Mrs. Conroy lifted the cover——"

"That is enough, Tom," said his mother. "We remember Uncle Edmund's tricks very well, and I've no doubt we'll soon see more of them."

But she looked forward to her younger brother's coming just the same, and when the pigeons came and there was no Uncle Edmund everyone felt surprised and concerned.

One night when they went to bed the sky was clear and the woods were still. But when they awoke in the crisp autumn morning the air was full of the noise of wings, and flocks of birds flew like clouds across the sun. The passenger pigeons were on their way south. They filled the trees in the woods. They came down in the fields and gardens, feeding on whatever seeds and grains they could find. The last birds kept flying over those which were feeding in front, in order to come at new ground, so that the flock seemed to roll along like a great moving cloud.

"The pigeons have come!" shouted the little Woodlawns. "The pigeons have come!" Even baby Joe
waved his arms and shouted.

Tom and Warren armed themselves with sticks and
went out with the hired men. But for once Caddie
stayed indoors. She liked hunting as well as the boys.
But this was too easy. This was not hunting—it was a
kind of wholesale slaughter. She knew that the Indians and the white men, too, caught the birds in nets
and sent them by thousands to the markets. She knew
that wherever the beautiful gray birds went, they
were harassed and driven away or killed. Something
of sadness filled her young heart, as if she knew that
they were a doomed race. The pigeons, like the Indians, were fighting a losing battle with the white
man.

But John Woodlawn was not a glutton as some of his
neighbors were. He said to Tom and the hired men:
"There is not much grain left in the fields now. Drive
the birds off and keep them from doing harm as well
as you can, but don't kill more than we can eat. There
is moderation in all things."

And so that night there was pigeon pie for supper.
But on the Woodlawn farm no more birds were killed
than could be eaten. After supper Robert Ireton,
strumming his banjo out by the barn, sang the song

that everybody had on his lips at this time of the year:

> *"When I can shoot my rifle clear*
> *At pigeons in the sky,*
> *I'll bid farewell to pork and beans*
> *And live on pigeon pie."*

The three children, huddled around him on the chilly ground, hummed or sang with him, and all about them in the darkness was the rustle and stir of wings.

A few days later the passenger pigeons had disappeared as suddenly as they had come. They had taken up their perilous journey toward the South. It was as if they had never passed by—except that the woods were stripped of seeds and acorns and dried berries, and some folks still had cold pigeon pie in their kitchens or dead birds on their truck heaps.

Then, after the pigeons were all gone, came a letter from Uncle Edmund announcing his arrival on the next steamer. The "Little Steamer," as everyone called it, came up the Menomonie River once a week as far as Dunnville. Its arrival was a great event, for all the letters from the East, all the news from the great world, most of the visitors and strangers and supplies came up the river on the Little Steamer.

The Woodlawn children begged to be allowed to go and meet Uncle Edmund.

"Certainly we can't take all of you!" said Mrs. Woodlawn calmly. "I shall let Clara and Tom go, because they are the eldest."

Tom looked at Caddie and Warren with a superior smile. "Too bad you little children have to stay at home," he said, "but we can't take all of you."

"All right for you, Tom," said Caddie, "talking like that!"

She and Warren withdrew. They crossed the barnyard and climbed to the haymow. Nero went with them to the bottom of the ladder. He was quick to sense trouble of any sort and his tail wagged in mournful sympathy. Caddie and Warren buried themselves in the hay and talked things over. When Father or Mother made a decision, the Woodlawn children accepted it as final. There was very little teasing for favors in a large pioneer family. But not to meet Uncle Edmund was unthinkable.

"It's just because they haven't room for us in the wagon," said Caddie at last, "but if we walked——"

"Sure," said Warren, his face brightening, "and let's not tell them we're walking either. Let's save it for a— a surprise."

"Or maybe we could take one of the horses," suggested Caddie.

"Pete's the fastest," said Warren.

"Better take Betsy. Pete always runs for the low shed behind the barn and scrapes us off."

"Sure," said Warren, "we'll take Betsy!"

When the time came to meet the steamer, Clara and Tom, in their Sunday clothes, climbed into the wagon behind Mr. and Mrs. Woodlawn. Tom was a little sorry for Caddie and Warren, but he couldn't resist a smirk of satisfaction. Only, strangely enough, Caddie and Warren did not seem as depressed over being left behind as they should have been. They stood beside the wagon, grinning like two Cheshire cats. Hetty and little Minnie stood with them, looking properly wistful. The moment the wagon started Caddie and Warren made a beeline for the barn to get old Betsy and ride across the fields and through the woods.

Hetty saw them go, and instant realization of what they were going to do flashed across her mind. Here was something important to tell. "Father! Mother!" she shouted, running down the lane behind the wagon. "Stop! Stop! Father! Mother!" But her voice was lost in the rattle of wheels, and in a cloud of dust the wagon disappeared. Across the field in the other direction flew Betsy, the black mare, with only a rope and halter, and Caddie and Warren clinging like monkeys to her bare back.

Dunnville consisted of the schoolhouse which the

children attended in winter and summer, a few log cabins, a store, and two taverns, one on either side of the river where the Little Steamer docked and turned around. As the Little Steamer came into sight, Mr. and Mrs. Woodlawn, Clara and Tom were standing on the dock ready with handkerchiefs to wave at sight of Uncle Edmund. Yes, Uncle Edmund was there. His round face was creased with smiles. His round eyes, behind his spectacles, twinkled with delight.

As soon as his voice could be heard over the sound of churning water, he shouted: "Hello there! Hello, Harriet and John! Hello, Tom and Clara! Hey, there, Caddie and Warren! Why don't you come on down?"

Caddie and Warren! The Woodlawns on the dock turned sharply around. There they were, Caddie and Warren, sitting on the bank above, their bare legs dangling, their red heads shining. They grinned sheepishly.

"Well, of all things!" cried Mrs. Woodlawn, her clear brow darkening ominously. She was going to say a great deal more, but suddenly the Little Steamer docked with a bump and she was obliged to catch her husband's arm to keep her balance. Then they were all in Uncle Edmund's large, enthusiastic embrace— even Caddie and Warren. Uncle Edmund was so delighted that they had all come to meet him that no-

body could bear to tell him it had not been planned that way.

As they were walking up the path from the dock, Uncle Edmund began to fumble in his pocket. "Wait," he said, "I've got a present here for Caddie."

Caddie stopped in her tracks, speechless with joy. The others crowded around them. Out of his pocket Uncle Edmund took a fat little book. Caddie had never felt much need of books, but any sort of present was a rare delight. She took the little book from Uncle Edmund's hand and opened the cover. Whiz! Something long and green flew out at her and fell into the path. Uncle Edmund shouted with laughter, and Caddie laughed, too, a little ruefully. She picked up the long green thing which lay in the path.

"That's no snake," she said. "It's got a clock spring inside it."

"Say, Uncle Edmund," cried Tom, "you'd ought to know you can't fool Caddie on snakes or clock springs. Try that on Hetty."

4 · A Silver Dollar

The next morning Uncle Edmund got out his gun and oiled and polished it. Then he polished his spectacles, for Uncle Edmund was near-sighted.

"Now," he said, "I've missed the pigeons, and that's a great pity, for a near-sighted man can always bring down a nice bag of pigeons. But I must do the best I can. Who will go with me to help me sight my game?"

Tom and Warren and Caddie stood beside him in breathless anticipation of this question. Uncle Edmund always asked it, and he always chose one of the three to go with him. More than one of them he would never take, for then, he said, they frightened the game away.

The three children spoke up with one voice: "I'll go, Uncle Edmund!"

Uncle Edmund looked them over critically. "Tom, you went last time I was here. You're pretty good, but you let a nice, fat squirrel get away. You remember?"

"Yah," said Tom, "but if I'd had the gun he wouldn't have got away."

"That's the trouble," said Uncle Edmund regretfully. "And Warren, here, talks too much. I might as well take a fife and drum corps."

"I wouldn't say a word," shouted Warren. "I wouldn't talk a bit. Just listen how quiet I could be."

"No," said Uncle Edmund, "I always have to fall back on Caddie in the end. I might as well start with her. She's as good as a pointer for showing me the game, and she never tells me how to shoot it nor reproaches me when I miss my aim. Come along, Caddie."

Caddie opened her mouth to speak. She was going to say: "It's too bad you little children have to stay at home. But, of course, we can't take all of you." But she closed it again without saying anything. After all, she did hate to see Tom and Warren disappointed, and also she didn't want to find a frog in her bed or a pail of water arranged over her door in such a way as to give her a drenching when she came back.

As she trotted along beside Uncle Edmund, she was

absolutely happy. It was perfect Indian-summer weather. The birch trees were all a-tremble with thinning gold. The oaks and sugar maples were putting on their vivid red and orange hues, and river, lake, and sky were all sublimely blue.

Uncle Edmund and Caddie struck across fields and through the woods to the lake. Nero went with them, for, although he had not been trained as a hunter, he loved to go hunting, and he had a strong affection for Uncle Edmund. Half drawn up on the shore of the lake were the Woodlawn children's two prized possessions—a homemade raft, of small logs or poles fastened together with wooden pins, and the Indian canoe hollowed from a single log. The little Woodlawns could manage almost any craft in any kind of weather, but, although they spent half of their time on either lake or river, they had never learned to swim.

Caddie ran ahead, her golden-red curls flying in the breeze. She threw her weight against the canoe and pushed it into the water. Then, her eyes shining with mischief, she jumped in and caught up the paddle.

"Beat you to the end of the lake, Uncle Edmund," she called. Uncle Edmund could swim, but he was no hand with a boat. He managed to get the raft afloat, and he and Nero scrambled aboard. Then he began to pole it down the lake. It swung from side to side and seemed to defy all of his attempts at steering.

"Hey, you little whippersnapper, you!" he shouted at Caddie, shaking his fist good-naturedly.

Caddie came back laughing and circled around the raft in her canoe. "Oh, I'm sorry, Uncle Edmund. Honestly I am. But I can't help laughing. You look so funny. You can take the canoe coming back, and I'll take the raft, and I'll beat you that way, too. See if I don't!"

"Oh, you'll beat me that way, too, will you?" said Uncle Edmund, a fine edge sounding in his voice. "How much will you bet?"

"Oh, I haven't any money and Mother doesn't like us to bet, but I'll beat you just the same."

"All right," said Uncle Edmund. "You won't bet, but I'll tell you what I'll do. If you can beat me coming back, I'll give you a silver dollar, that's what I'll do. Mind—you take the raft and I take the canoe."

"Bully for you!" cried Caddie, echoing Tom's favorite expression. She was confident of winning. A silver dollar! The Woodlawn children never had much money to spend, and, in those days of war-time "green-backs," a silver dollar was worth nearly three times the value of the paper dollar. Caddie was so delighted by Uncle Edmund's generosity that she offered to tow the raft to shore. But Uncle Edmund declined her offer and finally got himself awkwardly to the end of the lake. They beached their craft and started through the woods. But Uncle Edmund had forgotten something.

"Wait here a moment, Caddie. I left my game bag back on the raft."

"I'll get it, Uncle Edmund."

"No, wait here. I'll go myself."

Uncle Edmund was gone quite a long time, but at last he returned with the bag.

Now they went slowly and quietly, Uncle Edmund peering through his thick glasses at the nearby trees, Caddie's bright eyes searching the more distant places. Nero walked beside them, deeply excited. His business was sheep and cows, not game, but, as Edmund often said, a little training would have made him an admirable hunter. Suddenly Caddie stopped, her body stiffened, she put a tense hand on Uncle Edmund's arm.

"There!" she whispered, pointing to the branch of a tree some yards ahead. A squirrel sat there motionless, trying to look like a part of the tree. Uncle Edmund followed the direction of her finger with his near-sighted eyes. He raised his gun to his shoulder. Bang! The report reverberated through the woods, shattering the silence into a hundred echoes.

"I got him!" shouted Uncle Edmund exultantly.

"By golly, Caddie, I got him!" Caddie was as delighted as Uncle Edmund. She and Nero raced to
retrieve the squirrel for Uncle Edmund's game bag.

It was well along in the afternoon when they started
back toward the lake. Uncle Edmund was treading on
air, for he had three squirrels and a brace of par-
tridges, and, for a near-sighted man, that was a good
bag. Caddie's mind returned to the silver dollar she
was going to win.

"Remember, I'm going to beat you across the lake,
Uncle Edmund," she chirped.

"So you said. So you said," agreed Uncle Edmund
jovially, chuckling to himself. He sprang into the
canoe, and pushed off. Caddie thrust the raft into the
water and jumped on. Nero sprang on behind her, and
Caddie began to pole the raft. She and Tom had handled the raft so often that she knew just how to manage it to the best advantage. A few deft strokes
brought her alongside Uncle Edmund, who was hope-
lessly inefficient, even with such a delicate craft as a
canoe. But something curious was beginning to happen to the raft. One by one the small logs of which it
was built were beginning to float away. Caddie could
not believe her eyes. She poled for dear life, but the
faster she poled, the more quickly the logs fell away
from the raft. The space on which she stood grew
smaller and smaller. Someone had loosened all the

pins which held the raft together! Bit by bit it was coming apart.

"Uncle Edmund!" shouted Caddie, red with surprise and rage. Uncle Edmund lay back in the canoe and laughed. In a flash Caddie knew why Uncle Edmund had taken so long to fetch his game bag. The logs on which Nero stood came loose, and the old sheepdog plunged into the water and began to swim for shore. There were only three or four logs left together now and it took only an instant for them to drift apart. Caddie went down with a great splash, and her shining head disappeared beneath the water like a quenched flame. Presently she came up again, sputtering and blowing, and caught desperately at the nearest log. When she felt its rough surface under her fingers, she stopped struggling and clasped her arms about it. She was used to the feel of water up to her neck, if only she had something to hold onto. But she was angry. It took a good deal to arouse Caddie from her good nature, but every red-head's temper has its limitations, and Caddie's had been reached.

"Oh! Oh! Oh!" she sputtered, too angry to find any words.

Now that Uncle Edmund had had his little joke, he began to be worried. He brought the canoe around and helped Caddie into it. "Say, Caddie," he said, "I never thought that raft would come apart so quickly.

Honestly, I just wanted to scare you a little. You don't mind getting a little wet, do you? Just for fun?"

Caddie sat in the bottom of the canoe straight and stiff. Streams of water ran down all over her and made a puddle around her. Her face was pale and her hazel eyes flashed cold fire, but still she couldn't find a word to say to relieve her bottled indignation.

"Oh, say, Caddie, don't take it so hard," coaxed Uncle Edmund. "It was just a joke. Listen now, I'll give you that silver dollar I promised; but say, don't tell your mother, Caddie."

At last Caddie exploded.

"Are you trying to bribe a Woodlawn, Uncle Edmund?" she shouted. After everything else, to attempt to bribe a Woodlawn was heaping infamy upon infamy.

"Oh, no! no!" protested Uncle Edmund anxiously. "It's just a gift, Caddie."

"I wouldn't take it," cried Caddie. "I wouldn't take it if it was the last silver dollar in the world! I wouldn't——"

"Now, now, Caddie," urged Uncle Edmund. "Here we are almost to shore. Now, listen, you just take off your dress and dry it in the sun, and I'll go back and collect the pieces of the raft. That's a good, sensible little girl."

Caddie stepped out of the canoe with the haughty air of a scornful but dripping princess.

"You do as I say, Caddie," urged Uncle Edmund anxiously, "and I'll be back in half an hour with the raft." Caddie shook herself like a wet dog. Angry as she was, she realized that it was better to dry herself in the sheltered, sunny curve of the beach than to walk home through fields and woods in her dripping clothes. She wrung out her dress and petticoat and hung them on the bushes. Then she lay down in the warm sand. Presently Nero, who had made his way along the shore, came and sat beside her, drying his own coat in the sun.

Uncle Edmund was gone a long, long time. When he returned at last, Caddie was sitting in the sun in a dress that was wrinkled but dry. She had had time to think over her adventure, and her usual good humor had got the better of her anger. She burst out laughing when she saw Uncle Edmund's red, perspiring face. Poor Uncle Edmund had paid for his misdeeds.

"By golly, Caddie, that was a hard job. I've had my comeuppance-with, for once, my dear. But they're all here. I got every one." Behind the canoe he was towing the pieces of the raft, bound together with a rope which the children always kept in the bottom of the canoe. Caddie helped him pull the poles in to shore. He had managed to salvage most of the pins, too, and the two of them put the raft together once again.

"Well, I guess we're even, Uncle Edmund," said Caddie, gravely smiling. She held out her small, brown hand.

Uncle Edmund shook it heartily, but he said: "No, Caddie, we're not even yet. I promised you a silver dollar."

"You said if I beat you to the end of the lake on the raft, or if I wouldn't tell Mother. But I didn't beat you and I *am* going to tell Mother."

"Yes, yes, of course," said Uncle Edmund hastily, "but this dollar is just burning a hole in my pocket, my dear. Here, take it. It belongs to you."

Suddenly Caddie felt the weight of a silver dollar in the pocket of her dress. She put her hand in her pocket and the silver dollar felt warm and round to her fingers.

"Thank you, Uncle Edmund," she said.

They gathered up the game bag and the gun, and started for home. Their three figures were silhouetted against the sunset, Caddie, Nero, and Uncle Edmund, and their three shadows trailed far out behind them. Uncle Edmund, with a lulled conscience, was whistling. But Caddie's mind was busy with the many, many ways in which one could spend a silver dollar.

5 · Nero, Farewell!

"Say, I'd take a ducking every day in the week and twice on Sunday, for a silver dollar," remarked Tom enviously.

"Caddie, they've got bully tops in the store at Dunnville," added Warren hopefully.

Everybody had thought of a splendid way for Caddie to spend her dollar.

"You ought to buy yourself some gloves, Sister," said Clara. "You've never had proper ones and your hands look like an Indian's."

"Oh, Caddie, get a doll, please do," begged Hetty, "one of those china-headed ones with pink cheeks and blue eyes, and little china boots with high heels."

Little Minnie thought that the whole dollar should be spent on striped stick candy, and the boys were all for marbles and tops.

"Better keep it until Christmas, my child," advised Mrs. Woodlawn.

But Mr. Woodlawn said: "Leave the child alone. She has a wise head on her shoulders. She will know how to spend her money wisely when the time comes."

Caddie said nothing. But she put her dollar away in the little wooden trinket box which Father had made for her. Her head was full of plans—so many that she could not yet choose among them.

It was the evening before Uncle Edmund's departure. A sharp wind blew about the house, to remind them that even Indian summer must come to an end at last. Warm and cozy indoors, the Woodlawn family sat about the dining-room table. The supper cloth had been removed with the dishes, and a homespun cloth of red and white had taken its place with a lamp in the middle. The lamp was still rather wonderful to the little Woodlawns. They remembered when Father had first brought it home to replace the candles, and how they had all stood around to see it lighted and hear Father explain its use. Tonight by the light of the lamp Mrs. Woodlawn and Clara were darning, Mr. Woodlawn was mending a clock, and Uncle Edmund was cleaning his gun. The younger children sat about his feet near the fire, twisting bits of paper into the lighters which were used whenever possible instead of the precious sulphur matches.

Nero lay between Caddie and Uncle Edmund, his head pressed against Caddie's knee, his eyes opening from time to time to gaze in sleepy adoration at Uncle Edmund. He was completely happy here by the fire, between the two people he loved best. When he heard his name spoken, he raised his head and looked about. Uncle Edmund was saying: "There's one thing I want to ask you, Harriet. It's about Nero. Be a good sister, and let me take him back to St. Louis with me." Caddie and Tom sat up straight to listen. They stopped twisting lighters but they said nothing. They knew very well that when a grownup asked Mother a question, it was not their business to answer it, no matter how much they were interested.

"Why, Edmund," said Mother calmly, "whatever would you do with a sheepdog in St. Louis?"

"The point is, Nero's too good a dog for sheep. A little training and he'd be a fine bird dog. I know a chap who makes a business of training dogs. Nero would make me a splendid hunter, and you could easily get a new sheepdog."

"A good sheepdog requires as much training as a

bird dog, Edmund," said Mr. Woodlawn, "and to my mind he serves a worthier purpose."

"You have the mind of a farmer rather than a gentleman, John," said Uncle Edmund.

"Thank you, Edmund," replied Mr. Woodlawn gravely. "I appreciate that compliment more than you suspect."

"Come! come!" said Mother. "But surely, Edmund, you are not serious about taking Nero?"

"My heart is set on it, Harriet. You can see, yourself, how fond he is of me. I'll bring him back next fall, a perfect hunter."

"Oh, Uncle Edmund," Caddie couldn't help saying, "you *wouldn't* take him?"

"It would be for his own good, Caddie," said Uncle Edmund pompously. "He's a noble animal."

Caddie's fingers tightened in the thick wool on Nero's back. How many times she had felt its comforting warmth when things had gone wrong and she had needed comforting.

"No, Edmund, I am very much opposed to your taking him," said Mrs. Woodlawn.

"Now, Harriet, please," wheedled Uncle Edmund.

"You're so careless, Edmund. You nearly drowned my child last week. You'd be sure to let something happen to Nero."

"Now, listen, my dear." Uncle Edmund left his gun
and came to hang over the back of his sister's chair.
"I'll take perfectly good care of him. I'll bring him
back with me next fall. You know, Harriet, you never
could refuse your little brother anything he wanted."

"Dear! dear!" said Mrs. Woodlawn, settling her
white collar and smoothing her hair. "Do let me be.
You are worse than a mosquito, Edmund. John, what
shall I say to him?"

"It is for you and Edmund to decide, Harriet," said
Mr. Woodlawn.

"Well, then, take him," said Mrs. Woodlawn in an
irritated voice, "and take good care of him. I highly
disapprove, but you always have your way, Brother,
sooner or later."

"My dear, good sister!" cried Uncle Edmund. He
kissed Mrs. Woodlawn on the tip of her nose, and
began to do a bit of a sailor's hornpipe. Nero sprang up
barking, and the children were so enchanted by this
unaccustomed scene that they sprang up, too, laughing and quite forgetting the reason why they were so
gay.

They understood better the next day, when Uncle
Edmund went on board the Little Steamer with Nero
beside him on a leash. Nero jumped and barked, not
knowing what they meant to do with him. Caddie

knelt down beside him. Her face pressed against his rough coat, she clung to him a moment before Uncle Edmund led him away.

"Come back again, some day, Nero," she whispered. "Come back! come back!"

The Little Steamer chugged away downstream and a cold wind blew up the river in their faces. Uncle Edmund and Nero had a long journey ahead of them. Down the Menomonie River to the Chippewa, down the Chippewa to the Mississippi, down the Mississippi to St. Louis, where Uncle Edmund lived.

Tom and Caddie and Warren turned away from the dock and trudged back home to the farm. Somehow Uncle Edmund's visit had not been as satisfactory this year as they had expected. When they reached home, there was no welcoming bark, no Nero to greet them.

But it was too busy a time now to nurse regrets. There were the last wild grapes to pick, and butternuts and hazelnuts to gather. Tom, Caddie, and Warren were the fieldworkers of the family. They swung off across the fields and through the woods with buckets and baskets on their arms—three jolly comrades in search of adventure, in sunshine or frosty weather. Except for a few nutting expeditions, Clara and Hetty preferred to stay at home and help Mother with the sewing or quilting or jelly-making. As the autumn advanced the cranberries began to ripen in the marshes. Sometimes with the canoe, sometimes on foot, the three children pushed into the marshes to fill their buckets. It was dangerous going, for sometimes there was quicksand or quagmire in the marshes, and one must be quick and light of foot to leap from hummock to hummock, choosing the ground which would bear weight. Loons called and laughed their mirthless laughter over the marshes, and often a wedge of wild geese flew honking high overhead in the cold, blue sky.

"I'm getting dents in my thumb and finger, picking so many cranberries," complained Warren.

"I know," said Caddie. "Every time I close my eyes, I see millions of red berries swimming around."

"It's a good year for cranberries and for turkeys, too," said Tom. "I guess Mother will make a lot on her turkeys in market this year."

"Father says not. He says folks are too poor this year on account of the war to pay much for Thanksgiving turkeys."

"But Mother got more last year than she ever did before."

"I know, but Father says times are worse now, and she's got twice as many turkeys to sell."

"Well, I hope she keeps a few for us," said Warren, licking his lips. "Turkeys and cranberry sauce! Um—yum! She only let us have one for Thanksgiving last year."

The turkeys on the Woodlawn farm were Mrs. Woodlawn's own private enterprise. From the time that they were hatched, she watched over them with the most jealous care. She had never taken wholeheartedly to farm life, but she did have a real affection for her poultry. In her clean black and white sprigged calico, she stepped daintily about the poultry runs, with wheat or bran mash for some, and tidbits of chopped, boiled egg or soaked bread crumbs for the daintier appetites.

"Mother has a delicate hand with the fowls," Mr. Woodlawn used to say approvingly, and certainly her turkeys were the finest in all that rough, pioneer countryside. It was always a personal grief to her when a foolish young turkey swallowed a bee and died of a stung throat, and she swelled with a pride almost as great as his own when a fine cock with spread tail strutted by. This year she had the largest, finest flock that she had ever raised, and she would not listen to her husband's misgivings as to price. Away she had driven that very morning, all alone in the farm wagon with all her precious turkeys loaded on behind.

As the children returned that afternoon, their buckets heavy with cranberries, they saw her driving home. They ran to reach the farmyard as soon as she did. Mrs. Woodlawn drew up the horses silently. She had nothing to say, but the back of the farm wagon spoke for her. Gobble—gobble—gobble cried the wagonload of tired and hungry turkeys, who had come home again to roost.

"Why, Ma! You never sold your turks!" cried Tom, open-mouthed with astonishment.

"Tom Woodlawn!" cried his mother, "how many times have I told you not to call me 'Ma'!" She climbed down over the wagon wheel with the dignity of a great lady, but her lips were tightly compressed to hide their trembling.

"They are nothing but robbers there in town!" she cried. "They wouldn't give me enough for my beautiful birds to pay for rearing them. They said there was no market for them. No market for *my* birds! Ah, if I had these fine, plump fowls in Boston! Wouldn't I make a fortune? But out in this barbarous country all folks want to eat is salt pork. Poor trash! Poor trash!" She was trembling with anger and excitement.

Mr. Woodlawn stood in the barn door smiling quietly. Now he came out and put his arm about his wife. "Better luck next time, Harriet," he said.

"Oh, Johnny!" she cried and buried her head against his shoulder.

"But, Mother, what are you going to do with the turkeys if you can't sell them?" persisted Tom.

"We are going to eat them!" cried Mrs. Woodlawn, lifting a dauntless head from her husband's shoulder. "We'll hang them up and freeze them when the cold weather comes. We'll have roast turkey and cranberry sauce every day this winter!"

"Hooray!" shouted Caddie and Warren, waltzing each other around and around the barnyard.

"Hooray!" shouted Tom, imitating Uncle Edmund's hornpipe.

"Hooray! Hooray!" piped Hetty and little Minnie, running out of the house to hear what all the commotion was about.

Mrs. Conroy, who had come out at the first gobble of the returning turkeys, leaned her elbows on the fence and wagged her head.

"Faith and ye'll not be so plaised before th' winter's over," she said.

"Hush, Katie Conroy," cried her mistress. "They'll be tired of turkey soon enough, but let them enjoy themselves while they can."

"Hooray! Hooray! Hooray!" shouted the Woodlawn children.

6 · A Schoolroom Battle

These autumn days were busy ones indoors as well as
out. School would soon be starting for the winter, and
everyone must have the proper clothing. New dresses
and suits must be made, and old ones mended,
cleaned, and refitted to the younger children. Katie
Hyman's mother came out from the village to make
the dresses. She was a clever seamstress and had only
Katie's clothes to make, so she was glad of the extra
work which the Woodlawns could give her. Sometimes
yellow-haired Katie came with her. Sitting sedately
among the billows of brown and blue denim and
dotted challis, and stitching neat seams like her
mother's, she looked shyly at the Woodlawn children

from under her long lashes. They looked at her with
equal embarrassment. Such a quiet little girl, who
didn't ride horseback and was afraid of boys and
cows! They were not scornful of her. They simply
could not think of a thing to say to her. Only Tom, to
Caddie's great astonishment, once gave her an apple
and his best Indian arrowhead. Whoever would have
suspected Tom of that!

There were always blue and brown denim dresses
and suits for everyday. The Sunday clothes were more
exciting. They were made of nice, dark woolens, and
the girls had ruffly white aprons to wear over them.
What fun it was to try things on and turn about before
the mirror, while Mrs. Hyman, with her mouth full of
pins, begged you to stand still! The boys did not enjoy
the trying on so much. In fact Tom got all red and cross
when he had to be tried on with Katie Hyman sitting by. She scarcely looked up at all, but went on
stitching with her yellow curls falling down in front of
her face. But Tom would stumble over the footstool
that held the dish of pins, and his hands hung out of
the short, tight sleeves of the short, tight jacket, like
helpless sausages. That year there were wonderful
winter coats for the girls. They were made of red-and-
black checked woolen cloth which had been woven
from the wool of their own sheep. To make them even

finer, Father laid on the trimming braid himself. By the
evening lamplight, when he was not mending clocks,
he stitched the braid in place in neat and beautiful
designs. So the autumn slipped by and it was winter.
They were glad of the warm winter coats on the first
day of school, for snow had fallen in the night and
covered the ground with a thick white blanket.

"Why do we have to go to school in the coldest
weather?" complained Hetty. She was wrapped in a
muffler to the tip of her nose, and she had on a pair
of red woolen mittens which were fastened together
with a string around her neck under the red-and-black
checked coat. She and Caddie and the two boys were
walking across the snowy fields together; Clara had
finished school last year and little Minnie would not
start until next.

"It's because we're too poor to have a teacher to
ourselves all the year 'round," replied Caddie. "The
children of Durand have Teacher for spring and fall,
and we get her the rest of the time."

"And we're lucky, too!" said Tom. "If I've got to go
to school, I'd ruther go in winter when there isn't so
much fun outdoors."

"How about summer?" chimed Warren.

"Well, that's bad," admitted Tom, "but still I like
spring and fall the best for fun."

"Anyway," said Caddie, "it's only two months in summer and three in winter, and I like school."

"I'd like it, too, if it wasn't for Obediah Jones," said Hetty.

"If I was Teacher, I'd make those Jones boys behave," said Caddie.

"Teacher's scared of Obediah Jones," said Warren. "He's as big as she is and she dassn't lick him."

"I could lick him for her, if she'd let me," said Tom. "He needs it."

"I'll tell Mother if you go to fighting, Tom," warned Hetty in her piping voice.

"We'll wash your face in snow if you go bearing tales on Tom," countered Warren and Caddie.

Other muffled figures were coming across fields toward the little schoolhouse at Dunnville.

"Look!" shouted Caddie. "There's Maggie and Silas Bunn! Hey, Maggie, wait!" And she dashed off to catch her best friend, whom she had seen only once or twice since summer.

A column of blue smoke poured out of the schoolhouse chimney. Miss Parker, the teacher, with a shawl over her head and shoulders, stood in the doorway ringing a bell to hasten the feet of the stragglers. There was a great stamping of snowy feet in the woodshed and hall, and a clatter of lunch buckets and voices, as the children took off their wraps and hung them on the hooks. The one small room of the school-house was often cold, but today it was hot and filled with smoke from the newly started fire. The boys sat on one side and the girls on the other, about twenty children in all, and often varying in age from six to twenty-one. Some were well clothed and mannered. Others were almost as wild as the creatures that roamed the woods. Quiet and shy in a corner by themselves were Sam Hankinson's little half-breed children. They watched all that went on with bright, black eyes.

Caddie settled herself contentedly between Maggie Bunn and Lida Silbernagle with Jane Flusher just beyond. They were the four inseparables while school kept. Across the aisle the boys scuffled and whistled under their breaths. The teacher had her hands full with the boys of the Dunnville School. Some of them were as big as she was, or bigger, and they were used to the rough ways and the crude humor of a pioneer life. Ashur and Obediah Jones were the worst. Great, hulking boys who could scarcely get their knees beneath the desks, they came to school, not to learn, but to see what fun they could have baiting the teacher. Toward the end of the summer term, they had had things pretty much their own way, and they had returned now, full of vigor and anticipation. Obediah had worn his bearskin cap into the schoolroom, and now he stretched his long legs across the aisle and put his feet on Maggie Bunn's desk.

"Stop that, Obediah Jones!" cried Maggie. Her almost white pigtails quivered with indignation. Her good-natured blue eyes flashed dangerously.

"Who says so?" drawled Obediah, shoving his wet boots farther onto the desk.

"I'll tell Miss Parker, so I will!" cried Maggie.

"Tattletale! See if I care. I ain't scared of anybody in this school. Not me!"

"Is that so?" cried Caddie. She half rose in the bench beside Maggie and brought a large ruler down with all her strength across Obediah's shins. He was so taken by surprise that he yelped with pain, and brought his feet to the floor with a bang.

Instantly the schoolroom was in an uproar. Obediah lurched forward and caught hold of Caddie's curls, and Tom and Warren, sensing danger to Caddie, began leaping over benches and desks to get at her tormentor. But, if the Woodlawns were clannish, so were the Joneses. Ashur threw himself in Tom's way, and the two went down together, rolling and kicking, under the desks and benches. Clattering slates and the shrieks of frightened little girls mingled with the shouts of the boys.

Miss Parker, who had been calmly ringing the last bell, rushed in to behold her schoolroom in complete disorder.

"Boys! Girls!" she cried. "Stop! Stop at once!"

The noise began to die away. The shrieking girls and shouting boys slipped into their seats. Tom and Ashur ceased pommeling each other and crawled out from under the desks, looking a little ashamed of themselves. But in the middle of the room Caddie and Obediah still struggled and fought, Obediah pulling her curls this way and that and Caddie getting in a kick on his shins whenever she could. The children looked with awed faces from Miss Parker to the struggling pair. What would Miss Parker do? Her mouth had set in a hard, thin line.

"Obediah Jones! Caroline Woodlawn! Stop at once!" she cried, and she caught each one by a shoulder with firm hand. Obediah shook her off, but at the same time he let go of Caddie's hair, and with a well-directed parting kick Caddie let him go.

"What is the matter here? Who started this?" cried Miss Parker, her face pale and troubled.

There was an awful silence. Then Hetty, who must tell or burst, shouted: "It was Obediah, ma'am. He had his feet on Maggie's desk, and he wouldn't take them off. I saw him."

"Is this true, children?"

"Yes. Yes. It was Obediah, ma'am."

"And how did *you* get into it, Caddie?"

"Ma'am, he wouldn't take his feet off Maggie's desk and he said he wasn't scared of anybody in this school, and I hit his legs with a ruler."

"And I'm *not* scared neither," growled Obediah. "I kin do what I please and nobody dast stop me. I done what I pleased last summer and nobody dasted to stop me. Nobody dasts to stop me now." He set his bearskin cap straight on his head and looked at the teacher with defiant eyes. The teacher looked back at Obediah. She was a small woman, and now she was pale and trembling. It was a breathless moment. Even the youngest children knew instinctively that something was at stake. In a moment more they would find out whether Miss Parker or Obediah would rule the school this year.

Obediah began to grin—a slow, spreading grin. He pushed back his cap and spat contemptuously on the schoolroom floor. Then something polite and ladylike in Miss Parker snapped. She caught Obediah by the back of the neck with a suddenness that took him completely off his guard. Down the aisle she marched him to the front of the room.

"Obediah Jones," she cried, "I am going to punish you before the whole school. Stand up and take your medicine!"

"*I'll* lick him for you, ma'am," shouted Tom.

"No, Tom. Keep Ashur off, and leave the rest to me. It's Obediah or I now!" She whipped out her ruler, and laid it sharply across that section of Obediah's person on which he was accustomed to sit. For the second time that day he yelped with surprise and pain. He had a slow brain, and he had never really expected to have his authority questioned. When it finally dawned upon him that "teacher dast," he began to struggle. But he was too late. Miss Parker had already tasted the fruits of victory. She dealt him three more good smacks and then with a shake she let him go.

"Now, Obediah," she said, "go to the woodshed. You may either go home and never enter this schoolhouse again, or you may come back in five minutes and behave yourself like a gentleman the rest of the time you are here. Make your choice."

Obediah went out.

"Now, children," said Miss Parker, "start the multiplication tables."

They turned their scared faces toward the front of the room and began in wavering voices to sing the multiplication tables to the tune of "Yankee Doodle." Presently the woodshed door creaked a little on its hinges.

"Go right on singing. Don't look around," admonished Miss Parker crisply. Her pale cheeks were red now and she was no longer trembling. Through the thin sound of their singing, they heard Obediah coming slowly down the aisle. He had brought an armful of wood which he put carefully in the wood box. He had left his bearskin cap in the hall, and he had combed his hair. He sat down in his seat and folded his hands. Obediah had met his Waterloo, and Teacher was at last the greatest person in her little world.

7 · Attic Magic

The snow continued to fall and drifted high and deep. It was always warm indoors, and there was always turkey to eat. But sometimes out-of-doors it was too cold and the drifts too high for the children to walk to school. Then Robert Ireton hitched old Betsy to the sledge and drove them there. Their feet resting on heated stones, and wrapped in mufflers to the tips of their noses, the children huddled together to keep warm. The bells on Betsy's harness jingled, the runners creaked and groaned in the dry snow, and sometimes Robert Ireton sang:

"Say, Ike, did ye ever go into an Irishman's shanty?
Sure, it's there where the whiskey is plenty.
With his pipe in his gob, is Paddy so gay,
No king in his palace so happy as he.
There's a three-legged stool and a table to match,
And the door of the shanty it hooks with a latch.
There's a pig in the sty and a cow in the stable,
And, sure, they are fed of the scraps from the table.
They'd die if confined, but they roam at their 'ase
And come into the shanty wheniver they pl'ase.
   But say, Ike, Paddy's the boy!"

"Say, Ike, Paddy's the boy!" echoed the young
Woodlawns at the tops of their voices, above the jingling of the bells and the creaking of the runners.
Their breath rose in a steamy cloud from their singing mouths. The people in the village heard them coming, and said:

"It's them Woodlawn children, bless their souls!"

After the first tumultuous day, school had settled
into a quiet routine. Obediah was often sulky, but he
was no longer rebellious. Teacher had taught him his
lesson, and Ashur took his cue from Obediah. For
Caddie, the chief delight of school was the Saturday
morning spelling bee. On that day there was a review
of the week's work, and, after that, they could choose

sides for a spelldown. Each week the two best spellers, who stood out from the rest, were allowed to choose their teams for the next week. Caddie and Tom both had the sportsman's love of any test of skill. But Caddie was the better speller. She pored over the tattered spelling book with excited concentration, and she was usually the first to toss back her curls and fling up her hand to let Teacher know that she was ready to spell. She and Jane Flusher or Jane's brother Sam were usually the last ones standing at the end of the match, and then it was a fierce struggle to see which of them would go down first. The teacher had to turn to the back of the speller to "piccalilli" or "soliloquize" or "titillate," before either Caddie or the Flushers would be "spelled down" and have to take a seat in laughing confusion and defeat. As much rivalry entered into choosing the teams as in the actual spelldowns. The best spellers were promptly snapped up, and the worst ones left simmering in their shame until the end of the choosing.

Saturday afternoons were free. Sometimes the young Woodlawns went coasting or sleigh riding. Sometimes they all went with Tom to set traps for muskrats on the ice. Sometimes, and that was best of all, Father took Tom and Caddie and Warren with him to the mill at Eau Galle, and let them skate on the millpond. The ice froze there in a smooth sheet over the quiet pond, and only a little clearing of snow was needed to make good skating.

It was one Saturday late in December that Caddie came near drowning for the second time that year. Father had brought them to Eau Galle for the first skating of the season, and, while he was busy in the mill, Caddie and the two boys strapped on their skates and tried the ice. Tom was an expert skater, cutting figure-eights and scrolls and spirals in fine profusion over the new ice. Caddie and Warren were ambitious to do as well as Tom, but they could only follow along in awkward imitation of his skill. What they lacked in skill, they tried to make up in daring.

"You better be careful of that black ice," called Tom. "It's kinda thin looking."

"Who's afraid," laughed Caddie, and Warren said: "I dare you to see how far out you can go, Caddie."

"All right," said Caddie. "You can't scare *me!*" and away she went. The black ice began to creak and then to crack. Crash! Smash! Caddie was in over her head again! But what is only an adventure in a summer lake may be no joke in an ice-covered pond. Warren shrieked his alarm, but there was no time to fetch Father from the mill. Tom saw that only instant action on his part could save Caddie. With cool presence of mind, he made Warren lie down on the ice, and, catching hold of Warren's feet, he pushed him out over the thin ice until he could reach Caddie's groping hands.

"Hold tight, Warren," he shouted. "I'll pull you both in!" And he did. Nobody made much fuss over it. Pioneer children were always having mishaps, but they were expected to know how to use their heads in emergencies.

But it changed a large part of the winter for Caddie. Father dried her off as best he could in the engine room of the mill, wrapped her in buffalo robes, and drove her home. Mother put her into a steaming washtub before the kitchen fire, and then to bed with hot stones wrapped in flannel, and hot tea made of the dried leaves of wild strawberry plants. But Caddie had caught a bad cold, which kept her in bed for a week and home from school for several weeks after that.

Her mother sat on the foot of Caddie's bed the night of the accident, with a cup in one hand and a spoon in the other, and shook her head in despair. Exasperation and fond concern struggled on her pretty face.

"Caddie, why can't you behave like a young lady?" she sighed. "You'll be the death of me if not of yourself! Only a few weeks ago you were fighting with that awful Obediah Jones. Yes, Hetty told me about it.

And now you've nearly killed yourself skating on thin ice. If it isn't one thing, it's another!"

"I'm sorry, Mother," croaked Caddie hoarsely from the depths of a red-flannel bandage.

"Well, well," sighed Mrs. Woodlawn. "It seems to be your nature. What will you have for supper? A little turkey broth?"

Caddie sighed. "Isn't there any bean soup, Mother?"

"No, it's turkey, dear."

"Well, turkey then."

"That's a good girl. Go to sleep now."

Christmas came and went while Caddie was still recovering. She had intended to spend some of her silver dollar for presents, but it still lay snug and safe in the wooden trinket box, because she was not able to take it to the store. They hung their stockings by the fireplace on Christmas Eve and Santa Claus came down the chimney here in Wisconsin just as he did in Boston and St. Louis. But the apples and nuts which he packed around their toys were strangely like those which they themselves had picked.

"Mother," said Warren, "what are we going to have to eat for Christmas dinner?"

"Mince pie, Warren," said Mrs. Woodlawn brightly.

"That's good! But, I mean, what else?"

"Why, turkey and cranberries, of course! Folks always have that for Christmas dinner."

Warren sighed. "I know—but I thought, maybe—we'd have salt pork or something—just for a change."

"Now, Warren, you run along and play. There are plenty of folks who'd be glad of a good turkey dinner on Christmas! You should count your blessings!"

After Christmas Tom and Warren and Hetty went back to school, and the house seemed very empty. Caddie was not allowed to play with Minnie and baby Joe because of her cold, and when other household tasks were done, Mother and Clara were busy sewing carpet rags. Father was at the mill and Mrs. Conroy did not want to be bothered in her kitchen. Caddie looked at the family Bible and read Tom's dog-eared book of Andersen's *Fairy Tales*. She went into the parlor and looked at the Caroline table which really belonged to her, although Mother would scarcely let her touch it, for fear she might mar it. It had been made by one of Mother's ancestors for his wife, Caroline, and ever since that time it had come down to the Carolines of the family. Over it hung the silhouette of Great Aunt Kittie who had been the last Caroline before Caddie. But even a nice little mahogany table which really belongs to you isn't much company, and grows tiresome after you have looked at it for a while.

Caddie's wandering feet took her upstairs to the

attic. Here were old boxes from Boston, and a beautiful round-topped trunk, lined with colored paper, with pictures of smiling children decorating the various compartments. And on a low shelf was a row of clocks, waiting for Father's expert hand to mend them. The attic was drafty, but, near the head of the stairs, a big brick chimney came up from the kitchen, and there it was warm. Caddie drew some of the boxes over to the chimney and sat with her back against it, while she looked through them. Most of the things she had seen often enough. There were too many people in the family to allow old things to accumulate, un- used. Only two things which she found puzzled and surprised Caddie. She found them in the bottom of one of the boxes, and she knew that she had never seen them before. They were a pair of little red breeches and a pair of small, wooden-soled clogs. Surely they had never belonged either to Warren or to Tom. For some time they puzzled and excited her. Then she put them neatly away in the box, resolved to ask Mother about them as soon as she went downstairs.

Now she turned her attention to the clocks. They had been at the back of her mind all the time. She had been reserving them as a sort of final treat, as she often did with the things she liked best. She picked them up, one by one, and shook them to see if they

would start ticking. Among the others stood the circuit rider's clock. Caddie remembered what he had
said—it was the "face of a dead friend." Surely it
would soon be time for the circuit rider to return, and
Father had not yet started work upon the clock. How
dreadful it would be, if the circuit rider should return
and find his clock unmended! Caddie turned the clock
thoughtfully in her hands. She had seen Father mend
so many of them! Of course, they were not all alike
inside, but she knew how the little screws came out
and how the back came off, and then inside you saw
all of the fascinating wheels and gimcracks. Why
shouldn't she mend it herself? She was sure that she
could. She sat down with her back against the chimney
and began to loosen the screws.

It was more of a task than she had supposed. But
Father's tools were there on the shelf, and she found a
screwdriver of just the size she needed. The back came
off, revealing the wheels and springs. Caddie knew
enough about clocks to see what was the matter. The
circuit rider had wound his clock too tightly, and in
some way the spring had caught so that it could not
unwind as it should have done. Caddie looked it over
carefully. Then she began to loosen the screws which
held it in place. She had to loosen several before she
found the right ones. Time slipped away unheeded,

she was so deeply absorbed in the clock. Her cheeks were flushed and her face, bent low over her work, was curtained by her dangling curls.

And then at last she loosened the right screw! Whizz! bang! the spring flew out with a whirr and hit the low ceiling. Screws and cog wheels flew in every direction. It was like an explosion. The circuit rider's clock had suddenly flown to pieces! Caddie uttered a cry of despair and looked wildly about her. What would Father say?

There was a low chuckle from the stairway. Caddie followed the sound with startled eyes. Standing on one of the lower steps, so that his eyes were just above the level of the attic floor, stood her father. How long he had been watching her, she had no idea.

"Father," she wailed, "it went to pieces! The circuit rider's clock!" Her father leaned against the wall of the staircase and laughed. Caddie had almost never seen him laugh so hard. She, herself, did not know whether to laugh or cry.

"Father," she repeated, "it went to pieces!"

Still laughing, Mr. Woodlawn came up the stairs.

"Let's pick up the pieces," he said. "We're going to put that clock together, Caddie. I've been needing a partner in my clock business for a long time. I don't know why I never thought of you before!"

"A partner!" gasped Caddie. She began to race

about the attic, picking up screws and springs. "A real partner?"

"If you do well," said her father. "Clara is too busy with Mother, and Tom hasn't the patience nor the inclination. Yes, Caddie, I believe you'll be my partner."

Together they sat on the attic floor and put the circuit rider's clock in order. Mr. Woodlawn explained and demonstrated, while Caddie's eager fingers did the work. Together they cleaned and oiled the parts and made the nice adjustments that were required. By the time the work was finished, it was growing dark in the attic.

"Now take that down and show your mother, Caddie," said Mr. Woodlawn. Together they marched downstairs, one as proud as the other, and Caddie set the circuit rider's clock in the middle of the dining-room table.

"So you mended Mr. Tanner's clock, did you, Johnny?" said Mrs. Woodlawn carelessly.

"No, not this time," said her husband, with a twinkle in his eye. "Caddie did it."

"*Caddie did it?*" Mrs. Woodlawn and Clara and the children, who had just come in from school, crowded around to see.

"It runs," marveled Tom, and Warren uttered an admiring "Golly!"

The circuit rider's clock no longer looked like the "face of a dead friend." It appeared to be very much alive and spoke up with a cheerful tick.

Caddie never forgot the lesson she had learned that day in the attic. Wherever she was, all through her long and busy life, clocks ticked about her pleasantly, and, if they didn't, she knew the reason why.

8 · Breeches and Clogs

The long winter evenings in the farmhouse were very pleasant times. Grouped about the fire and the lamp, the Woodlawns made their own society, nor wanted any better. One evening soon after Caddie's adventure in the attic, they were all gathered together thus. Everyone who belonged was there—except Nero. Caddie missed the faithful head resting against her knee. They were recalling old adventures that they had had, and now Clara was speaking in her gentle voice.

"Yes," she said, "it was the first winter we were out here. We lived at Eau Galle then, near the mill, and we had school in the tavern. Caddie and Tom were little then, and Warren was a baby."

"Where was *I*?" demanded Hetty.

"You hadn't come yet."

"Go on and tell," urged the other children. They all sat about the big stove, cracking butternuts between hammer and stones, and dropping the meats into a wooden bowl.

"There isn't much to tell," continued Clara in her soft voice, "only I came through the woods one day and I saw a bear eating a little pig."

"Where did he get it?" asked Warren.

"From one of the farms, I guess."

"Were you scared?" asked Hetty.

"Oh!" said Clara, putting her slim hand against her heart. "I was so scared. It makes my heart thump yet to think of it!"

"I wouldn't have been so scared," boasted Tom. "Remember, Caddie, when we saw the wolves?"

"*Uh-huh!*" said Caddie, her mouth full of butternuts.

"Tell about that," said Warren. "I wish I'd been there."

"Well, one time the cows got into the swamp, and Caddie and I went after them to bring them home, and right in the swamp we met a wolf."

"Did he bite you?" asked little Minnie breathlessly.

"No, he just stood and looked at us, and we looked at him."

"I'd have shot him or hit him with a rock," said Warren.

"You hold your tongue, Warren," said Tom. "I guess you'd have done the same as us, if you'd been there. I don't know what would have happened next, if two big hounds hadn't come along and chased him away."

"Aw, you're making it up," said Warren, who was always skeptical of any adventures which Tom and Caddie had without him.

"No, honest," said Tom. "Caddie will tell you the same thing. The hounds were after him—that's why he acted so funny. They belonged to a man down the river."

"Robert Ireton can tell a better one than that," said Warren. "He says there was a fiddler coming home through the woods late one night from a dance, and a pack of wolves took after him. He saw he couldn't get away from them, so he stopped and played his fiddle to them, and they all went away and let him go home in peace."

"I know!" said Tom. "It's true, too. Robert had it from a man who married the fiddler's sister."

Mr. Woodlawn smiled at his wife and said: "Ireton knows how to tell a good story as well as sing a good song, I see."

Caddie had been listening to the stories in silence. Now she suddenly jumped up, shaking the nutshells from her apron into the wood basket. Without a word, she caught up one of the candles which burned on a side table and ran upstairs to the attic. She hastily went through the contents of one of the boxes until she found what she was seeking; and downstairs she ran again, almost before the others had ceased gaping over her sudden departure.

"Look!" she said. She held up a small pair of scarlet breeches and two little wooden-soled clogs.

"Well, of all things!" cried Mrs. Woodlawn. "Wherever did you get those?"

"In one of the boxes in the attic."

"What are they? What are they?" cried the children, leaving their nuts to crowd nearer.

"I don't know whose they are," said Caddie. "There must be a story about them, Mother. Do you know it?"

Mrs. Woodlawn looked at her husband. He had taken one of the little shoes in his hand, and it scarcely covered his big palm. He turned it this way and that, smiling an odd, perplexed smile.

"Well, well, well!" he said. "What a funny little shoe!"

The impatient children crowded nearer, and little Minnie clambered onto his knee.

"Father," cried Caddie, "you know something about them! Tell us!"

"Tell us! Tell us!" echoed the others.

"Yes, Johnny, you had better tell them now," said Mrs. Woodlawn.

Mr. Woodlawn still hesitated, his eyes deep with thoughts of something far away, something beyond the warm room and the ring of bright, expectant faces; something less bright and warm and happy.

Mrs. Woodlawn stirred impatiently. "Those are your father's shoes, children," she said. "He used to dance in them in England, and the little red breeches, too—long, long ago. Do tell them, Johnny. They've a right to know."

"Yes, yes," said Mr. Woodlawn, "they have a right to know and I have always meant to tell them. But it's a long story, children, you had best go back to your hassocks and your nuts."

Eyes round with wonder and anticipation, the young Woodlawns did as they were told. To think of Father ever being small enough to wear those breeches and clogs, and dancing in them, too, in faraway England. How strange it was! They had heard so much of Boston, but nobody spoke of England where the strange little boy, who had grown to be Father, had danced in red breeches and clogs. Caddie thought of what Father had said about England on the night when the circuit rider had been with them. How often she had wondered about that since then!

"You have grown up in a free country, children," began Mr. Woodlawn. "Whatever happens I want you to think of yourselves as young Americans, and I want you to be proud of that. It is difficult to tell you about England, because there all men are not free to pursue their own lives in their own ways. Some men live like princes, while other men must beg for the very crusts that keep them alive."

"And your father's father was one of those who live like princes, children," cried Mrs. Woodlawn proudly.

"My father was the second son in a proud, old family," said Mr. Woodlawn. He set the clock he was mending beside him on the table, and his hands, unaccustomed to idleness, rested awkwardly on his knees. "My father's father was a lord of England, and the lands he owned rolled over hills and valleys and through woods."

"Bigger than ours?" wondered Hetty.

"Many times. Yes, many, many times. There was a great stone house with towers and turrets and a moat with swans, and there were peacocks on the lawn."

"Peacocks!" cried Clara, clasping her hands.

"Yes," said the father gravely. "I saw them once

when I was a little boy. My mother held me by the hand and I stood on tiptoe to look between the bars of the great gate, and there they were, a dozen of them, stepping daintily, with arched necks, and spreading or trailing their great tails upon the grass."

"But, Father," said Caddie, "why were you outside?"

"Well may you ask that question, Caddie!" cried Mrs. Woodlawn. Her earrings trembled with her indignation.

"Old Lord Woodlawn was very proud," said Father, "and he had planned a brilliant future for his second son. . . . Thomas, my father's name was—that's where you get your name, Tom. But Thomas Woodlawn wanted to live his own life, and he had fallen in love. His heart had overlooked all the fine young ladies of high degree, and had settled upon the little seamstress who embroidered and mended and stitched away all day in the sewing room of the great house."

"Just like Tom and Kat—" began Hetty, but Caddie suddenly thrust a butternut into her mouth, and the rest of what she had intended to say was lost.

"I cannot blame him for falling in love," said Father. "That little seamstress was very beautiful and sweet. She was my mother. They were married secretly, and then they went to old Lord Woodlawn and told him. They thought that he would forgive them, after it was done and past repair. But they hadn't reckoned on the old man's stubbornness and wounded pride. You see, my mother was the daughter of the village shoemaker. God knows, the old shoemaker earned an honest living and lived an upright life, but to my Grandfather Woodlawn's notion anything connected with such a trade was low and shameful."

"How funny!" said Caddie, "if he was a *good* shoemaker."

"The old lord was beside himself with anger. He ordered Father to forsake his bride, but that my father would not do, so the old man turned them out together. 'Never come back,' he told my father. 'You are no longer my son.' If my father had been the eldest son, the laws of England would have restored his position to him at the death of the old lord. But a disinherited second son has nothing to look forward to. So now he found himself penniless and with a wife to support."

"But I don't understand!" said Caddie.

"No, my dear," said her father. "It is hard to understand an old man's selfish pride. He had planned his son's life, and he could not endure to have his plans lightly set aside. He might have taken my father back if Father had forsaken Mother, but that was not my father's way. And so the two young things went out into the world to make a living for themselves. My father had been trained to ride a horse to hounds, to read a little Latin, and to grace a drawing room, but he knew no more about any useful trade than baby Joe. There was one thing he could do, however. He had always had some skill at drawing and painting, and, as a boy, his father had humored him by letting him have lessons in the art. Now he found that he could get occasional work by painting panels and murals in taverns and public houses. It was a sorry comedown for the son of a nobleman. Sometimes they paid him only in food and lodging and he and his wife were obliged to stay there eating and sleeping out his earnings. Truly they were glad enough to have a roof over their heads and something in their stomachs, I imagine. I, myself, remember the long walks and the slim dinners and sometimes nights spent under a haycock, when we could not find a tavern which wanted decorating."

"Poor Father!" cried Caddie softly.

"But worse was to come," said Mr. Woodlawn slowly. "The tramping about, the worry and hunger and cold were too much for my father, who did not have the peasant hardiness of my mother and me. I was about ten years old when he died, and I was a little lad who looked scarce half my years."

"And what did you do then?" breathed the little Woodlawns anxiously.

"My mother had no money to take us home again,

and what could she have expected for us if she had
gone? The old lord was not likely to forgive her after
his son was dead, and the shoemaker was as annoyed
with his daughter for marrying out of her class as the
old lord was himself. And then my mother had her
own amount of pride. In those days the worst vice in
England was pride, I guess—the worst vice of all,
because folks thought it was a virtue."

"But, Father, what about the clogs and breeches?"
asked Caddie.

"Have patience," said Mrs. Woodlawn. "He'll get to
them presently."

"My mother earned what she could as a seamstress.
But that was not enough. We had no home of our own
and we wandered from lodgings to lodgings always
half-hungry and owing money. I did what odd jobs I
could, but folks thought me too small and young to be
entrusted with much. I was a lively lad, as gay as a
cricket, in spite of my troubles. I had learned to dance
and I begged my mother for a pair of clogs. The poor,
good woman had no money to spare for dancing clogs,
as I well know now. But, I daresay, I left her no
peace, and suddenly she had an idea for granting my
request and at the same time adding something to our
income. She bought me the clogs and made me a little
green jacket and a pair of red breeches. There was a
green cap, too, with a red feather, and so I danced,

and people threw me coppers as if I had been a monkey."

"Did you make a lot of money, Father?"

"No, but I made enough to help a bit, and sometimes they even engaged me in cheap music halls to do a week's turn or two. That was a great event."

"Oh, Father, can you still dance?" cried Caddie.

"I've still got two legs," said Mr. Woodlawn, gay once more.

"Oh, do! do!" the children cried, seizing him by the hands and pulling him out of his chair.

"Oh, Father, dance! Do!"

Mr. Woodlawn laughed. Then suddenly he pursed his lips and began to whistle an old-fashioned jig. Tap! tap! tap! went toe and heel, and suddenly he was jigging and clogging and snapping his fingers to the astonishment of the open-mouthed children. They formed a delighted ring about him, clapping and shouting, and keeping time with their feet.

Mrs. Woodlawn got up quickly and went into her bedroom. Nobody missed her, nor heard her opening the drawers in the chest where the linen was kept. When the dance was over, and Father sank, breathless and laughing, into his chair, Mrs. Woodlawn came out with a small oil painting in her hands.

"Your father will never show you this," she said, "so I am going to."

"No, no, Harriet," begged Mr. Woodlawn, still laughing and panting. "It's too foolish."

"The children shall judge of that," said his wife, and she propped the canvas up on the table. It was a dim picture, painted in an old style, of a very funny little boy. The little boy seemed scarcely more than a baby and he was dressed in a quaint little sailor suit with a wide-brimmed hat. Two tufts of bright red hair were pulled down on either side of the face, beneath the brim of the hat. Everybody began to laugh. And yet there was something sad and wistful, too, in the eyes of the strange little boy who looked at them.

"It's your father," said Mrs. Woodlawn, "and it was *his* poor, dear father who painted it. Your father was only three years old."

The children shouted with laughter, but Caddie felt a little bit as if she wanted to cry, too, and she reached for Father's hand and squeezed it.

"It's a wicked shame!" continued Mrs. Woodlawn tartly. "All that land in England, that great stone house, even the peacocks—they ought to belong in part to your father, perhaps entirely. Who knows? Think, children, all of you might have been lords and ladies!"

"No, no, Harriet," said Mr. Woodlawn, growing grave again. "It was a hard struggle, but what I have in life I have earned with my own hands. I have done well, and I have an honest man's honest pride. I want no lands and honors which I have not won by my own good sense and industry."

Just then the clocks all over the house began to chime ten.

"Ah! my dears!" cried Mrs. Woodlawn. "When have you ever gone so late to bed! Scamper now, as fast as you can!"

Frightened by the idea of sitting up so late, the little children scurried to obey. Clara and Caddie went more slowly upstairs together. Clara's slender shoulders were lifted with a new pride and her dark eyes shone.

"Peacocks on the lawn, Caddie," she whispered. "Just think!"

"Peacocks!" repeated Caddie softly, and then suddenly she scowled and clenched her fists. For she was seeing the peacocks through a great, barred gate, with a funny little boy in a sailor suit and a wide-brimmed hat, whose wistful eyes looked sadly out between his odd tufts of red hair.

9 · "The Rose Is Red"

Caddie went back to school again in February. Her long vacation had grown tiresome. Even the excitement of finding the breeches and clogs and of hearing Father's story, even the delight of being Father's partner in business, did not make up for the long, lonely hours when the other children were at school. She was glad to be back at school in time for Valentine's Day, for that was always fun. On that day most of the children exchanged comics, but you could tell which boys had "sweethearts," because their fancies betrayed them into paper lace and true love knots, turtle doves, and clasped hands.

Tom had been pensive for several days before Valentine's Day.

"Golly, Caddie," he said one day, "if I had a silver dollar like you have! Say, why don't you spend it for Valentines?"

"A whole silver dollar for Valentines!" cried Caddie, her thrifty soul sincerely shocked. She felt a little superior to Tom, because she knew that he could never save his money.

"Well, maybe not *all* of it," said Tom. "But, say, you just ought to see the beauties they've got down to Dunnville store."

Caddie considered the matter. It did not occur to her that possibly Tom was hinting at a loan. But she had kept her dollar for so long now that she had grown a little miserly. She had saved six pennies besides her silver dollar, and these she took out and put in her pocket on February thirteenth. After school that day, with her pennies jingling pleasantly in her pocket, she started for the Dunnville store. Hetty, who had bought hers weeks in advance, and Warren, who thought that Valentines were silly, trudged home across the fields. But where was Tom? He had been the first one out of the schoolhouse and now he was nowhere to be seen. Caddie broke into a trot, and, just as she came in sight of the Dunnville store, she saw a familiar figure disappearing into the back door. Tom! But why the back door? And why was Tom so mysterious these days?

Caddie went in and chose six penny comics. One for Tom, one for Warren, one for Hetty, and the rest for Maggie, Jane, and Lida Silbernagle. Then she stood transfixed at the sight of the most beautiful Valentine that she had ever seen. It was propped up against a tobacco jar, so that everyone could admire it. It was all paper lace and roses and violets, and in the center of a pink heart was printed:

> *The rose is red,*
> *The violet's blue,*
> *Sugar is sweet,*
> *And so are you.*

Caddie almost regretted that she had left her dollar at home. This was so beautiful! Still she wouldn't know to whom to give it. *She* wasn't "sweet on" anybody.

"How much is it?" she asked the storekeeper just to satisfy her curiosity.

"Two bits," Mr. Adams replied with a twinkle in his eyes, "but I guess it's sold, Caddie. There's a young man in the back room here sprouting potatoes for it."

"Oh!" said Caddie. Now she knew. It was Tom! But was it for her, this lovely Valentine? It seemed impossible. Tom always gave her the rudest kind of comics, and she thought them fun. Yet who was a better friend to Tom than she? No one, surely. She went home slowly, wondering. She knew that Tom wouldn't want anyone to know that he was sprouting potatoes to earn a Valentine, so she locked his secret in her heart. It was the first one she had ever known him to have from her.

The next day the schoolhouse was full of titters and whisperings. Miss Parker resigned herself to keep what order she could. Valentine's Day was a day to be got through as best one might, and she was glad that it came only once a year.

Mysterious envelopes and scraps of paper kept appearing on desks; children squirmed excitedly in their seats. Silas Bunn even upset an inkwell over his sister Maggie's taffy-colored pigtail, in an effort to punch the boy who had given him a picture of a donkey sitting on a dunce's stool.

Caddie hastily scanned her Valentines. She hadn't expected the "rose is red" one, and yet she couldn't help looking to make sure. But it wasn't there. The comic ones were very funny, though, and there was a little bag of candy hearts from Sam Flusher, who held no hard feelings even if she did beat him sometimes in spelldowns. Altogether it was a good day.

At morning recess someone slipped in and hung a slate on the front of Teacher's desk. On it were drawn long two-legged, skinny creatures with heads like buttons, labeled Teecher and Obediah. They were fighting, and around them was drawn a heart. Teacher, not having occasion to go in front of her desk and see it, attributed the unusual amount of giggling to the influence of the day. But Obediah had to sit gazing at the slate with growing fury until noon. At noon, as soon as Miss Parker had gone into the hallway for her lunch basket, Obediah seized the slate in his big hands and broke it into four pieces which he flung into the stove. He glared around the room without saying a word and then stalked outdoors. Obediah was tamed, but the children saw with awe that he was still a lion at heart.

Still the "rose is red" Valentine did not appear, and Caddie began to wonder if Tom had got tired of sprouting potatoes before it was won. Then, when they came in from afternoon recess, she saw it, lying in a square, white envelope on Katie Hyman's desk. Surely she had known that it would be there all the time. Katie saw it, too, and blushed and shook her curls over her face. It was the first Valentine that she had had that day, for she was so shy that no one dared to give her penny comics. Her little pale, slim fingers, that were so quick with the needle, trembled as she opened it, and then everybody who had gathered around said: "Oh!" for they recognized it at once as the best Valentine in the Dunnville store. Katie turned it

around and looked all over it, but there was no name on it anywhere. She was smiling more than they had ever seen her smile, and her eyes sparkled, almost as if they had tears in them. Caddie looked at Tom, but he was standing by the stove finishing an apple, and talking with some of the boys, as if he had never heard of Valentines in his life.

After school Hetty was all excited.

"Caddie, did you see that great big Valentine Katie Hyman got? Who do you suppose sent it? There wasn't any name, but I'm sure that Tom sent it. Don't you think so? I'm going to tell everybody so."

Caddie's heart jumped. If Hetty told, they would make Tom's life miserable.

"Why, Hetty," she said gayly, putting her arm around the walking newspaper. "Whatever put that in your head? You know Tom can't save a cent. Then how do you suppose he could buy the finest Valentine in the store without any money?"

"That's so," said Hetty. "I know! Maybe she got it for herself, just to make folks think she had a beau."

Busy with this happy thought, Hetty broke into a run. Caddie walked along more slowly. She was thinking: "I do everything with Tom. I'm much more fun than Katie. Why, she's afraid of horses and snakes and she wouldn't cross the river for worlds. I don't believe she's spoken three words to Tom in her life. But she's what you call a little lady, and I'm just a tomboy. Maybe there's something in this lady business after all."

But just then Warren caught up with her and said: "Hey, let's go coasting! All this silly Valentine, sugar-plum stuff!" And she raced away with him, laughing, and eager to be the first one on the hill with her sled.

The ever-increasing trial that the little Woodlawns had to endure this winter was turkey. How far away now seemed that autumn day when they had capered and danced, shouting: "Turkey every day! Hooray! Hooray! Hooray!"

When the school lunches were being packed, one of the boys was sure to appear and say: "Ma, I mean Mother, what're we going to have in our bread today?"

Sometimes Mrs. Woodlawn said brown sugar or jelly, but usually the answer was: "Cold turkey, dear."

"Oh, that!"

"There's nothing nicer than turkey on bread, my child. Think of all the poor children who would be glad of a nice turkey sandwich!"

Tom and Caddie and Warren had often thought of these poor children who had no turkey. Secretly they envied them. One can endure beef every day, or even salt pork. One eats it mechanically, without thinking, but *not* turkey. No matter how disguised with onions or cabbage, or sage dressing, turkey is always turkey.

One day Tom made a valuable discovery. The little half-breed Hankinsons brought buckets of parched corn to school for lunch. Now that they were tired of turkey, there was nothing the Woodlawns liked better than parched corn. Undoubtedly, Tom said, the Hankinsons were the poor children Mother meant, who would be glad of a nice turkey sandwich. The little Hankinsons looked hungrily at the beautiful slices of white bread which were the pride of Mother and Mrs. Conroy. They sniffed the delicate aroma of roast turkey.

Upon Tom's advice, Caddie made the first advances. "How would you like a piece of white bread and some turkey, Gussie?" she said to the eldest boy, holding out a sandwich temptingly. Gussie's black eyes sparkled in his brown face. In all his nine years, he had never been offered a piece of white bread with turkey in it. Jerked venison, they had at home, and salt pork, but his mother cooked as the Indians did, and his father was too indolent to try to teach her the white man's way of preparing food. The two little brothers crowded close to Gussie, and the youngest one held out his hand.

"You give us parched corn," said Caddie, "we give you turkey bread."

"We do," said Gussie, and the three little Hankinsons ran to get their pails of parched corn. After that it was easily arranged. Whenever the Woodlawns had turkey in their lunch, they traded buckets with the Hankinsons, and everyone was happy.

Caddie's birthday was on February 22, the same as George Washington's. There were too many of the young Woodlawns for anyone to make a fuss over their birthdays. It was pleasant enough to be alive, without thinking to celebrate the day on which one had begun to be so. But with Caddie it was a little different—not at home, of course. But at school, Teacher hung up a flag and there were songs and speeches.

"I know they're not for me, exactly," Caddie confided to Tom, "and yet I guess I enjoy them more than George Washington does."

Teacher said that President Lincoln had his birthday in February, too, and Caddie wished more than ever that she had been a boy. Perhaps she could have grown up to be a president then, but now she would have to leave that to Tom or Warren.

This year Miss Parker let Caddie hold the flag while the others sang. She stood straight and proud at the front of the room beside Miss Parker's desk, her eyes

on the lovely stars and stripes—Mr. Lincoln's flag, the
flag of the North, Caddie Woodlawn's flag.

> *"Oh, say, can you see,*
> *By the dawn's early light . . ."*

Her heart always soared with the familiar words and
seemed to break in a shower of delight on "How
proud-ly we hailed." All about her she saw the sparkle
of "bombs bursting in air," beautiful bombs that
would not hurt anyone. She thought of Father, looking through the barred gate at peacocks on an English
lawn, and she lifted her head, saying fiercely to
herself:

"I love America more than Maggie Bunn or Lida or
Jane! I'm more American than all of them, because—
because they were unkind to Father in England."

10 · *Hoofs in the Dark*

That afternoon, when they came home from school, the snow was melting in a sudden thaw, and the sky was blue above the bare branches of the trees. Caddie skipped as she walked, still feeling the high elation she had felt as she held the flag. Twelve years old she was. Time to begin to be a young lady, Mother said. But Caddie did not think so, and Father's smiling eyes were still on her side.

"Give the child time, Harriet. Give the child time," he had said at breakfast. "We are long enough grown up, my dear, when the time comes. Let the child get her health."

"Health!" sniffed Mother. "She's simply bursting

with it! When I was her age, I could make bread and jelly and six kinds of cakes, including plum, not to mention all the samplers I had stitched which anyone may see if they care to look in my marriage chest. And what does Caddie know how to do?"

"I can plow," said Caddie with a twinkle in her eye, for she knew that her mother was not as indignant as she sounded.

"Plow!" exclaimed Mrs. Woodlawn, rolling her eyes and holding up her hands. "Yes, my daughter knows how to plow!"

"Let her have a little more time, Mother," said Mr. Woodlawn quietly. "She'll see her way soon."

But, when they reached home, the conversation of the morning had been entirely forgotten. Mrs. Woodlawn stood by the kitchen window with an abstracted look on her face. Her sleeves were rolled up as if she had been about to make biscuits, and in her hand she held an open letter. As the children entered, Mrs. Conroy was wiping a tear from the corner of her eye with her apron.

" 'Tis too bad, Mum," she was saying, "and him so good and faithful, too, and never would touch pork, neither, but looked at me so reproachful-like whiniver I offered it to him. Poor love!" Mrs. Woodlawn turned at the sound of the children's entrance. There was something tender and sad in her face for them, and she went up and kissed each one on the forehead. Most often she was too busy about her household to greet them with kisses when they came in from school.

"What is it, Mother?" asked Caddie, sensing something wrong.

"It's a letter from Uncle Edmund, Caddie," replied her mother slowly. "I must tell you children that I was wrong to let Edmund take Nero. I knew it at the time, but I let him persuade me."

"*Mother!*"

"Uncle Edmund says that Nero is lost, that he was very unhappy in the city, that he has run away." There was a little catch in her usually calm, crisp voice. She held out the letter.

"Nero won't come back next fall with Uncle Edmund?" cried Tom, unable to accept this news.

"No, Tom, Nero is lost," repeated Mother.

Caddie snatched the letter and read. It was all as Mother said.

Terribly sorry, Harriet [the letter ran], *I shouldn't have taken him, I suppose, but one doesn't foresee such things. He was most unhappy here in the city. Missed the sheep and the children probably. I kept him tied, but one day he got away and was gone like a streak. I assure you that I have done everything in my power to find him. It is several weeks now since he left and I have only now given up hope of finding him. I write all this with the greatest regret, for I know how fond you all were of Nero. When I come in the fall, I shall try to bring a puppy with me to take his place.*

"A *puppy!*" cried Caddie, flinging the letter down and setting her muddy foot upon it. "A *puppy*—any old puppy—to take the place of Nero!" She burst into tears and rushed upstairs to throw herself onto her bed and bury her head in her pillow, where her sobs could not be heard by the others. All the loneliness she had felt for Nero since he had gone away overwhelmed her now in a great flood. Nero, whose eyes full of sympathy, whose wagging tail and warm tongue had always sustained her in her moments of unhappiness and doubt, Nero was gone, and now she would never see him again. Worst of all, Nero had been lonely for her. He had been unhappy and frightened in the city. The thought of that hurt Caddie more than her own loneliness.

Mrs. Woodlawn came up and sat on the foot of her bed. "I am sure, Caddie," she said softly, "that he will find a good home. Anybody would like Nero, and he could soon find his way to a farm where there are sheep and children."

But Caddie was inconsolable.

When they came up again to fetch Caddie down to supper, she was sound asleep, worn out with crying. Mother thought it best to let her sleep as long as she would.

It was only when Hetty and Minnie came to bed that Caddie roused herself. She felt stiff and cold and a little dazed. But she was extremely hungry. She went downstairs and stood by the dining-room fire, warming her back and rubbing her hands together. On a corner of the table nearest the fire Mother had spread a napkin over the red and white checked homespun cloth. A place for one was neatly laid, and there was a bowl of warm milk, a plate of bread, a nicely polished red apple, and a plate of cold meat. It was *not* turkey. All of the children had gone to bed, only Father and Mother sat on beside the fire, each busy with some evening occupation.

"Sit down, dear, and eat," said Mother quietly.

Caddie obeyed, and there was no other sound in the room but the ticking of clocks and the occasional crackling of the fire. But something warm and peaceful and comforting seemed to flow through the quiet room and make everything right again.

Caddie had just finished eating and was about to place one of the silver spoons which Mother had brought with her from Boston on the plate beside her

bowl. Instead, she held it suspended a moment in the air while she listened. There was another sound in the quiet room. It was the distant sound of hoofbeats on the road. Father and Mother had heard it, too. Father went to the window and looked out. Mother sat still, listening, her face turned toward the road from Dunnville, her knitting needles idle in her lap. People did not ride abroad at night in February without some good reason in those days. The sound of hoofs came more distinctly now. Someone was riding rapidly in spite of the darkness.

"They're coming here," said Mrs. Woodlawn, jumping up. "One of the neighbors is sick, perhaps. I must get my shawl and bonnet."

The hoofs sounded to the very door, then stopped. Then someone was knocking, loudly and urgently, on the door. Father went and opened it. A cold wind blew in and Caddie could see the pale face of a man beyond Father's shoulder. She brought the lamp to light them. The man was Melvin Kent from the other side of Dunnville.

"I don't want to alarm you, Woodlawn," he said, "but there's a serious rumor going around. The Indians—"

"Just a moment, Kent," said Father, and he stepped outside and closed the door behind him.

Caddie set the lamp again on the table. Mother had come back with her shawl and bonnet. She and Caddie looked at each other silently, their eyes frightened and questioning. They stood together near the table, listening to the rumble of men's voices outside. All the peace and friendly security of the quiet room had flown out into the February darkness when Father had opened the door.

It seemed a very long time before Father came back. His face was grave, but outwardly he was as calm as usual.

"What is it, Johnny? What is it?" cried Mrs. Woodlawn, unable to bear the suspense any longer.

"Nothing serious, I hope," said her husband, laying his hand absently along Caddie's shoulder as he spoke. "A man from the country west of here came into the tavern tonight and told the men that the Indians are gathering for an uprising against us."

"*Massacre!*" breathed Mother, laying her hands against her heart. Her face had gone quite white.

"No, Harriet, not that word," said Father quietly. "Not yet. I hope that this is only a tavern rumor and nothing more. Many a fool who has had too much to drink will start a rumor. I am willing to stake my farm, and a good deal that I hold dear besides, on the honor and friendliness of the Indians hereabouts. Still, we must keep clear heads and be ready for emergencies. Whatever happens, the white settlers must stand together. I have told Kent that the neighbors may gather here."

"Yes, yes!" said Mrs. Woodlawn. "We can house them better than anyone. How soon will they come?"

"They'll begin to arrive by daybreak, I imagine." The white look left Mrs. Woodlawn's face. Now there was something to be done! "Daybreak!" she said. She looked at the clock. It was ten minutes past eleven.

"I'll call Katie Conroy and we'll begin to bake," she cried. "No telling how long they'll be here, and they'll be hungry. We can shake down pallet beds in the parlor for the women and children. The men can bunk in the hay, if those wicked redskins don't fire it before they have a chance to bunk. Fetch me six strings of dried apples from the storeroom, Johnny, and a bucket of water from the spring. I know! We can use up some of the turkeys on the neighbors! I am sure 'twill be a great treat to them as are not accustomed to excellent fowls, excellently cooked. Besides, if this thaw continues, my beautiful birds will be lost, and, Heaven knows, if the savages come, I wouldn't have *them* eat my turkeys! What, Caddie! Are you still here? Get to bed as fast as you can, child. I'll call you at daybreak."

11 · Massacree!

In those days the word massacre filled the white settlers with terror. Only two years before, the Indians of
Minnesota had killed a thousand white people, burning their houses and destroying their crops. The town
of New Ulm had been almost entirely destroyed.
Other smaller uprisings throughout the Northwest
flared up from time to time, and only a breath of rumor
was needed to throw the settlers of Wisconsin into a
panic of apprehension.

"The Indians are coming! The Indians are coming!"
Without waiting to hear more, people packed what
belongings they could carry and started the long
journey back East. Others armed themselves as best

they could for the attack and gathered together in groups, knowing that there was strength in numbers. Sometimes, leaving the women and children at home, the men went out to attack the Indians, preferring to strike first rather than be scalped in their beds later. The fear spread like a disease, nourished on rumors and race hatred. For many years now the whites had lived at peace with the Indians of western Wisconsin, but so great was this disease of fear that even a tavern rumor could spread it like an epidemic throughout the country.

By daybreak the next morning people began arriving at the Woodlawn farm from all directions. They came bringing what food and bedding they could carry. They did not know how soon they would dare return to their homes, nor whether they would find anything but a heap of charred sticks when they did return. Of course, school was not to be thought of, and, in spite of the general fear, the children were delighted with the unexpected holiday.

With shouts of joy the young Woodlawns greeted Maggie and Silas Bunn, Jane and Sam Flusher, and Lida Silbernagle. Katie and her mother came, too. Katie's eyes were round with alarm, and she kept close in the shadow of her mother's hoop skirt. Both of them were quiet, asking nothing but protection. The

other children played I Spy around the barn and farmyard, their pleasure keenly edged by the nearness of
danger. An exciting game became much more exciting
when, on coming out of hiding, one felt that he might
find himself face to face with a redskin instead of tow-
headed Maggie or gentle Sam.

Mrs. Woodlawn was in her element. She loved a
gathering of people, and one of her great griefs in
Wisconsin was that she saw so few outside her own
family. Now she had all the neighbors here, and could
herself serve them beans such as none but she, outside
of Boston, knew how to bake, and slices of turkey
which had their proper due of praise at last. Happy in
the necessity of the moment, she did not let her mind
dwell on the danger from the Indians.

Clara worked beside her mother, her thin cheeks red
with excitement, her capable hands doing as much as a
woman's. Caddie helped, too, but, after she had
broken a dish and spilled applesauce over the kitchen
floor, her mother told her that she had better run and
play, and Caddie ran. Flinging her arms over her head,
she let out an Indian war whoop that set the whole
farm in an uproar for a moment. Women screamed.
Men ran for guns.

"Aw, it's only Caddie," said Tom, "letting off
steam."

"Put a clothespin on her mouth," suggested Warren.

But Caddie did not need a clothespin now. The men with their guns looked too grim to risk another war whoop on them.

The day wore slowly on, and nothing unusual happened. The children tired of their games and sat together in the barn, huddled in the hay for warmth, talking together in low voices.

"You 'member the time the sun got dark, eclipse Father called it, and we were so scared? We thought the world had come to an end, and we fell down on our faces. You 'member?"

"Yah. We saw a bear in a tree that day, too. Remember?"

"Golly! Do you think the Indians'll come tonight?"

"Maybe they will."

"I don't dast to go to sleep."

Their voices trailed off, lower and lower, almost to whispers.

The night came, gray and quiet, slipping uneventfully into darkness. The February air had a hint of spring in it. Would the promise of spring ever be fulfilled for them? Or would the Indians come?

Mr. Woodlawn's calm voice sounded among the excited people. "I believe that we are safe," he said. "I trust our Indians."

Caddie's heart felt warm and secure again when she heard him speak. Tom and Robert Ireton went among the people, too, repeating Father's words. But others were not so easily reassured.

"It's well enough for *you* to talk, Robert Ireton," cried one of the women who was holding a baby wrapped in her shawl. "If the Indians come, you young men can get away in a hurry. You haven't any children or stock or goods to hold you back."

"Lady," said Robert in his rich Irish voice, "if the Indians come, sure, we young men will not be getting away in a hurry. We'll be here by your sides and fighting to the finish."

Caddie heard him say it, and straightened her shoulders like his. She could be as proud of Robert Ireton as she was of Father.

After dark, sentries were stationed about the farmhouse to keep watch during the night, and the women and children made their beds on the floor of the parlor, after the bedrooms were filled. No one undressed that night, and fires were kept burning in the kitchen and dining room for the men to warm by when they changed their sentry duty. Windows were shuttered and lanterns covered or shaded when carried outside. A deep silence settled over the farm. They did not wish to draw the Indians' attention by needless noise or light.

But the night passed as the day had passed and nothing fearful happened. The children awoke stiff and aching and rubbed the sleep out of their eyes, surprised to find themselves lying in such queer places. Caddie had given her bed to old Grandma Culver, and she was as stiff and tired as any of them. But the good cows had not been frightened out of giving their milk, and Robert Ireton, humming a tune, brought in two foaming buckets of it for the children to eat with the big bowls of meal mush which Mother and Mrs. Conroy ladled out of a great iron pot. The stiffness and queerness vanished like magic with the comfort of hot mush and milk—even if one did have to stand up to eat it.

But the second day was worse than the first. People were restless and undecided. Should they go home or should they stay on? The food supplies they had brought with them were giving out. They could not let the Woodlawns exhaust all their supplies in feeding them. Yet the redskins might only be awaiting the moment when they should scatter again to their homes to begin the attack. It was a gray, dark day, not designed to lift anybody's spirits. A fine mist, almost but not quite like rain, hung in the air and curtained all horizons in obscurity.

The women and little children, crowded into the farmhouse, were restless and tired of confinement.

The men paced back and forth in the farmyard, or stopped in groups beneath the four pine trees that sheltered the front of the house, and which Father had named for Clara, Tom, Caddie, and Warren. The men polished and cleaned and oiled their guns, smoked their pipes, and spat into the mud which their boots had churned in the tidy dooryard. Everyone felt that the strain of waiting had become almost unbearable.

In the afternoon a few of the men went to get more supplies. Tom, Warren, and Father went with them. The others watched them go, fearful and yet somehow relieved to see any stir of life along the road.

Caddie felt the strain of waiting, too, and she was impatient with the people who had no faith in the Indians. The Indians had not yet come to kill. Why should they come at all? Indian John had never been anything but a friend. Why should he turn against them now? Why should his people wish to kill hers? It was against all reason. Good John, who had brought her so many gifts! Why should not everyone go home now and forget this ugly rumor which had started in the tavern?

"Caddie," said Mrs. Woodlawn, "go fetch me a basket of turnips from the cellar, please." Caddie slipped on her coat, took up the basket and went outside where the cellar door sloped back against the ground at the side of the house. She had to brush by a group of men to get into the cellar. They were talking earnestly together, their faces dark with anger and excitement.

"It is plagued irksome to wait," one of them was saying as Caddie brushed past.

She went into the cellar and filled her basket. "Yes, it's irksome to wait," she said to herself, "but I don't know what they mean to do about it. They'd be sorry enough if the Indians came."

But what they meant to do about it was suddenly plain to her as she came up the stairs again with the turnips.

"The thing to do is to attack the Indians first," one man was saying. It was the man Kent, who had ridden out on the first night to spread the alarm. Caddie stopped still in her tracks, listening unashamed.

"Yes," said a second man. "Before they come for us, let us strike hard. I know where John and his Indians are camped up the river. Let's wipe them out. The country would be better without them, and then we could sleep peacefully in our beds at night."

"But the rumor came from farther West. Killing John's tribe would not destroy the danger," objected a third man.

"It would be a beginning. If we kill or drive these

Indians out, it will be a warning to the others that we deal hard with redskins here."

Caddie set her basket down upon the stair. It suddenly seemed too heavy for her to hold. Massacre! Were the whites to massacre the Indians then? A sick feeling swept across her heart. Surely this was worse than the other. As if her thought had occurred to the first speaker, but in a more agreeable light, he said: "Let them say the men of Dunnville massacree the Indians, instead of waiting to be massacreed!"

"Woodlawn will be against it," said the more cautious third man.

"Woodlawn puts too much faith in the Indians. If we can get enough men to our way of thinking, we need not consult Woodlawn. I don't believe in caution when our lives are in danger. Wipe the Indians out, is what I say. Don't wait for them to come and scalp us. Are you with me?"

White and trembling, Caddie slipped past them. The men paid no attention to the little girl who had left her basket of turnips standing on the cellar steps. They went on talking angrily among themselves, enjoying the sound of their boastful words. Caddie went to the barn and into the stalls. There she hesitated a moment. Pete was faster than Betsy, but he was not so trustworthy. When he didn't want to go, he would run

under a shed or low branch and scrape off his rider.
Nothing must delay her today. Caddie slipped a bridle
over Betsy's head. She was trembling all over. There
was something she must do now, and she was afraid.
She must warn John and his Indians. She was certain
in her heart that they meant the whites no harm, and
the whites were going to kill them. Good John, who
had given her the little calico and buckskin doll with
its coarse horsehair braids!

Oh, for Tom and Warren now! But they were gone
with the men for supplies. Oh, for Father, who was
always so wise and brave! But she could not wait for
him to come back to tell him what he would never believe about his neighbors, unless he had heard it himself. There was no use going to Mother or Clara. They
would only cry out in alarm and forbid her to go, and,
since Father and the boys were not here, she felt that
she must go. She knew as well as Kent where Indian
John and his tribe had built their winter huts of bark.
Fortunately, for the moment the barn was deserted.
She must go while there was still time and before anybody saw her. She led Betsy to the little back door that
opened toward the river. There was only one field to
cross there and then she would be in the woods. The
barn would shut off the sight of her departure from the
house and the road.

She had her hand on the latch of the door, when someone said: "Caddie!"

Caddie's hazel eyes blazed black in her white face as she turned. But it was only Katie Hyman who had followed her into the barn. Katie's delicate face, framed in its pale halo of hair, was full of alarm.

"Caddie, what are you doing? Where are you going?"

"Oh, Katie," said Caddie with a choking noise like a sob, "they're going to kill John and his Indians because he hasn't come to kill us. I've got to warn him."

"You wouldn't go to the Indians *now!*" said Katie. "Oh, Caddie, no! You *couldn't* do that!"

"I've got to!" said Caddie grimly. "They must have a chance to get away. Don't tell a soul where I've gone, Katie. Cross your heart!"

Katie hesitated, her eyes wide with terror. Caddie had always been the leader at school. It was impossible for gentle Katie to disobey her. Her fingers made a feeble crisscross in the direction of her heart.

"Cross my heart," Katie whispered.

Caddie flung herself on Betsy's back and dug heels into her flanks. She was away across the field and into the dripping wood. The gray mist was turning into fine rain. There was still snow in the wood and there would still be ice on the river.

Katie shivered. She closed the small barn door and stood still with both hands pressed against her heart. An old cat, who had kittens in the loft, came by on noiseless feet, a dead mouse hanging from her mouth. She stared back, her own eyes round with fear.

"I crossed my heart," she whispered.

12 · Ambassador
to the Enemy

Clip-clop-clip sounded Betsy's hoofs across the field.
There was a treacherous slime of mud on the surface,
but underneath it the clods were still frozen as hard
as iron. Then the bare branches of the woods were all
around them, and Caddie had to duck and dodge to
save her eyes and her hair. Here the February thaw
had not succeeded in clearing the snow. It stretched
gray and dreary underfoot, treacherously rotted about
the roots of big trees. Caddie slowed her mare's pace
and guided her carefully now. She did not want to lose
precious time in floundering about in melting snow.
Straight for the river she went. If the ice still held,
she could get across here, and the going would be

easier on the other side. Not a squirrel or a bird stirred
in the woods. So silent! So silent! Only the clip-clop-
clip of Betsy's hoofs.

Then the river stretched out before her, a long ex-
panse of blue-gray ice under the gray sky.

"Carefully now, Betsy. Take it slowly, old girl."
Caddie held a tight rein with one hand and stroked
the horse's neck with the other. "That's a good girl.
Take it slowly." Down the bank they went, delicately
onto the ice. Betsy flung up her head, her nostrils dis-
tended. Her hind legs slipped on the ice and for a
quivering instant she struggled for her balance. Then
she found her pace. Slowly, cautiously, she went daintily forward, picking her way, but with a snort of disapproval for the wisdom of her young mistress. The ice
creaked, but it was still sound enough to bear their
weight. They reached the other side and scrambled up
the bank. Well, so much done! Now for more woods.

There was no proper sunset that day, only a sudden,
lemon-colored rift in the clouds in the west. Then the
clouds closed together again and darkness began to
fall. The ride was long, but at last it was over.

Blue with cold, Caddie rode into the clearing where
the Indians had built their winter huts. Dogs ran at
her, barking, and there was a warm smell of smoke in
the air. A fire was blazing in the center of the clear-

ing. Dark figures moved about it. Were they in war
paint and feathers? Caddie's heart pounded as she
drew Betsy to a stop. But, no, surely they were only
old women bending over cooking pots. The running
figures were children, coming now to swarm about her.
There was no war paint! no feathers! Surely she and
Father had been right! Tears began to trickle down
Caddie's cold cheeks. Now the men were coming out
of the bark huts. More and more Indians kept coming
toward her. But they were not angry, only full of
wonder.

"John," said Caddie, in a strange little voice, which
she hardly recognized as hers. "Where is John? I must
see John."

"John," repeated the Indians, recognizing the name
the white men had given to one of their braves. They
spoke with strange sounds among themselves, then one
of them went running. Caddie sat on her horse, half-
dazed, cold to the bone, but happy inside. The Indians
were not on the warpath, they were not preparing an
attack. Whatever the tribes farther west might be
plotting, these Indians, whom Father and she trusted,
were going about their business peacefully. If they
could only get away now in time, before the white men
came to kill them! Or, perhaps she could get home
again in time to stop the white men from making the

attack. Would those men whom she had heard talking by the cellar door believe a little girl when she told them that Indian John's tribe was at peace? She did not know. Savages were savages, but what could one expect of civilized men who plotted massacre?

Indian John's tall figure came toward her from one of the huts. His step was unhurried and his eyes were unsurprised.

"You lost, Missee Red Hair?" he inquired.

"No, no," said Caddie, "I am not lost, John. But I must tell you. Some white men are coming to kill you. You and your people must go away. You must not fight. You must go away. I have told you."

"You cold," said John. He lifted Caddie off her horse and led her to the fire.

"No understan'," said John, shaking his head in perplexity. "Speak too quick, Missee Red Hair."

Caddie tried again, speaking more slowly. "I came to tell you. Some bad men wish to kill you and your people. You must go away, John. My father is your friend. I came to warn you."

"Red Beard, he send?" asked John.

"No, my father did not send me," said Caddie. "No one knows that I have come. You must take your people and go away."

"You hungry?" John asked her and mutely Caddie

nodded her head. Tears were running again and her teeth were chattering. John spoke to the squaws, standing motionless about the fire. Instantly they moved to do his bidding. One spread a buffalo skin for her to sit on. Another ladled something hot and tasty into a cup without a handle, a cup which had doubtless come from some settler's cabin. Caddie grasped the hot cup between her cold hands and drank. A little trickle of warmth seemed to go all over her body. She stretched her hands to the fire. Her tears stopped running and her teeth stopped chattering. She let the Indian children, who had come up behind her, touch her hair without flicking it away from them. John's dog came and lay down near her, wagging his tail.

"You tell John 'gain," said John, squatting beside her in the firelight.

Caddie began again, slowly. She told how the whites had heard that the Indians were coming to kill. She told how her father and she had not believed. She told how some of the people had become restless and planned to attack the Indians first. She begged John to go away with his tribe while there was still time. When she had finished John grunted and continued to sit on, looking into the fire. She did not know whether he had yet understood her. All about the fire were row on row of dark faces, looking at her steadily

with wonder but no understanding. John knew more
English than any of them, and yet, it seemed, he did
not understand. Patiently she began again to explain.

But now John shook his head. He rose and stood tall
in the firelight above the little white girl. "You come,"
he said.

Caddie rose uncertainly. She saw that it was quite
dark now outside the ring of firelight, and a fine,
sharp sleet was hissing down into the fire. John spoke
in his own tongue to the Indians. What he was telling
them she could not say, but their faces did not change.
One ran to lead Betsy to the fire and another brought
a spotted Indian pony that had been tethered at the
edge of the clearing.

"Now we go," said the Indian.

"I will go back alone," said Caddie, speaking distinctly. "You and your people must make ready to
travel westward."

"Red Hair has spoken," said John. "John's people
go tomorrow." He lifted her onto her horse's back, and
himself sprang onto the pony. Caddie was frightened
again, frightened of the dark and cold, and uncertain
of what John meant to do.

"I can go alone, John," she said.

"John go, too," said the Indian.

He turned his pony into the faint woods trail by

which she had come. Betsy, her head drooping under a slack rein, followed the spotted pony among the dark trees. Farther and farther behind, they left the warm, bright glow of fire. Looking back, Caddie saw it twinkling like a bright star. It was something warm and friendly in a world of darkness and sleet and sudden, icy branches. From the bright star of the Indian fire, Caddie's mind leaped forward to the bright warmth of home. They would have missed her by now. Would Katie tell where she had gone? Would they be able to understand why she had done as she had?

She bent forward against Betsy's neck, hiding her face from the sharp needles of sleet. It seemed a very long way back. But at last the branches no longer caught at her skirts. Caddie raised her head and saw that they had come out on the open river bank. She urged Betsy forward beside the Indian pony.

"John you must go back now. I can find my way home. They would kill you if they saw you."

John only grunted. He set his moccasined heels into the pony's flanks, and led the way onto the ice. Betsy shook herself with a kind of shiver all through her body, as if she were saying, "No! no! no!" But Caddie's stiff fingers pulled the rein tight and made her go. The wind came down the bare sweep of the river with tremendous force, cutting and lashing them with the sleet. Betsy slipped and went to her knees, but she was up again at once and on her way across the ice. Caddie had lost the feeling of her own discomfort in fear for John. If a white man saw him riding toward the farm tonight, he would probably shoot without a moment's warning. Did John understand that? Was it courage or ignorance that kept John's figure so straight, riding erect in the blowing weather?

"John!" she cried. But the wind carried her voice away. "John!" But he did not turn his head.

Up the bank, through the woods, to the edge of the clearing they rode, Indian file. Then the Indian pony stopped.

Caddie drew Betsy in beside him. "Thank you!" she panted. "Thank you, John, for bringing me home. Go, now. Go quickly." Her frightened eyes swept the farmstead. It was not dark and silent as it had been the night before. Lanterns were flashing here and there, people were moving about, voices were calling.

"They're starting out after the Indians!" thought Caddie. "Father hasn't been able to stop them. They're going to massacre."

She laid her cold hand on the spotted pony's neck. "John!" she cried. "John, you must go quickly now!"

"John go," said the Indian, turning his horse.

But, before the Indian could turn back into the

woods, a man had sprung out of the darkness and caught his bridle rein.

"Stop! Who are you? Where are you going?" The words snapped out like the cracking of a whip, but Caddie knew the voice.

"Father!" she cried. "Father! It's me. It's Caddie!"

"You, Caddie? Thank God!" His voice was full of warm relief. "Hey, Robert, bring the lantern. We've found her. Caddie! My little girl!"

Suddenly Father was holding her close in his arms, his beard prickling her cheek, and over his shoulder she could see Robert Ireton with a bobbing lantern that threw odd shafts of moving light among the trees. John, too, had dismounted from his pony, and stood straight and still, his arms folded across his chest.

"Oh, Father," cried Caddie, remembering again her mission and the last uncomfortable hours. "Father, don't let them kill John! Don't let them do anything bad to the Indians. The Indians are our friends, Father, truly they are. I've been to the camp and seen them. They mean us no harm."

"You went to the Indian camp, Caroline?"

"Yes, Father."

"That was a dangerous thing to do, my child."

"Yes, Father, but Kent and some of the men meant to go and kill them. I heard them say so. They said they wouldn't tell you they were going, and you weren't there. Oh, Father, what else could I do?"

He was silent for a moment, and Caddie stood beside him, shivering, and oppressed by the weight of his disapproval. In the swaying lantern light she searched the faces of the three men—Robert's honest mouth open in astonishment, Father's brows knit in thought, John's dark face impassive and remote with no one knew what thoughts passing behind it.

Caddie could bear the silence no longer. "Father, the Indians are our friends," she repeated.

"Is this true, John?" asked Father.

"Yes, true, Red Beard," answered John gravely.

"My people fear yours, John. Many times I have told them that you are our friends. They do not always believe."

"My people foolish sometime, too," said John. "Not now. They no kill white. Red Beard my friend."

"He brought me home, Father," said Caddie. "You must not let them kill him."

"No, no, Caddie. There shall be no killing tonight, nor any more, I hope, forever."

Over her head the white man and the red man clasped hands.

"I keep the peace, John," said Father. "The white men shall be your brothers."

"Red Beard has spoken. John's people keep the peace."

For a moment they stood silent, their hands clasped in the clasp of friendship, their heads held high like two proud chieftains. Then John turned to his pony. He gathered the slack reins, sprang on the pony's back and rode away into the darkness.

"Oh, my little girl," said Father. "You have given us a bad four hours. But it was worth it. Yes, it was worth it, for now we have John's word that there will be peace."

"But, Father, what about our own men? They meant to kill the Indians. I heard them."

"Those men are cowards at heart, Caddie. Their plans reached my ears when I got home, and I made short work of such notions. Well, well, you are shivering, my dear. We must get you home to a fire. I don't know what your mother will have to say to you, Caddie."

But, when they reached the farmhouse, the excitement of Caddie's return was overshadowed by another occurrence. Katie, who had sat pale and silent in a corner all during the search, rushed out of the house at the sound of Caddie's return.

"Caddie!" she cried, "Caddie!" Then suddenly she crumpled like a wilted flower, and had to be carried away to bed.

In the excitement of fetching smelling salts and water, Mrs. Woodlawn had only time to cry: "Caddie, my dear. You ought to be spanked. But I haven't time to do it now. There's a bowl of hot soup for you on the back of the stove."

In the kitchen Tom, Warren, Hetty, Maggie, and Silas, all the children, crowded around Caddie as she ate, gazing at her in silent admiration, as at a stranger from a far country.

"Golly, Caddie, didn't they try to scalp you?"

"Did they have on their war paint?"

"Did they wave their tomahawks at you?"

Caddie shook her head and smiled. She was so warm, so happy to be at home, so sleepy. . . .

13 · Scalp Belt

The day after Caddie's ride to the Indian camp, life settled into the old routine. The neighbors went home again. No charred black ruins awaited them. The sturdy wilderness houses were just as they had left them, only dearer than ever before, and in the log barns hungry cows bawled lustily for food.

Everyone recognized now that the "massacree scare," which had started in the tavern, had been a false alarm. But the terror which it had inspired was not easily forgotten. Many people left the country for good, making their slow way eastward, their few possessions piled high in wagon or cart, their weary cows walking behind. Tales of bravery or cowardice during

the "scare" were told and retold around the winter
fires and, at last, people were able to laugh at them
instead of trembling. One of the tales the people of
Dunnville loved best was of the fiery old man upriver,
who, although past sixty, left his old wife to defend
the homestead with the only gun they owned, while he
set out empty-handed to fight the Indians.

But, although it all came to nothing and folks could
laugh at the "massacree scare" at last, still it left with
many people a deeper fear and hatred of the Indians
than they had ever felt before. The Indians themselves
understood this. Now that the excitement was over,
they were safe from even the most cowardly of the
white men. But, nevertheless, they prepared to leave
their bark huts and move westward for a time. They
felt the stirring of the sap in the trees. A smell of
spring in the winter air lured them. The old women
made bundles of their furs and blankets and cooking
pots and put them on pole and buckskin litters. The
ponies pranced, the dogs barked. The Indian men refitted bowstrings, polished knives and guns, and prepared the canoes for a long portage over the ice.

One day, soon after the "scare," when Caddie came
home from school, she saw an Indian pony tied to the
rail fence near the kitchen door. Clara ran out of the
front door to meet her.

"Oh, Caddie," she said, "do hurry. Indian John's in the kitchen and he wants to see you. He won't say a thing to the rest of us. Father's away and Mother and Mrs. Conroy are nearly frightened out of their wits. He's got his horrible old dog with him and his scalp belt, too."

Caddie ran around the house and opened the kitchen door. Between the cook stove and the table sat John, bolt upright, with a large piece of dried apple pie in each hand. Solemnly he bit into first one piece and then the other, Mother and Mrs. Conroy peeping timidly at him from the dining-room door the while. His scalp belt lay on the kitchen table beside the empty pie tin and the clean fork and plate which city-bred Mother had laid for him so daintily. At his feet lay his dog, licking its front paw with a slow red tongue.

"Why, John, I'm glad to see you," said Caddie. She stooped and patted his dog. The dog stopped licking his paw for a moment and looked at Caddie with affectionate eyes.

"Him hurt," said John. "Him caught foot in trap."

Caddie bent closer over the foot. "Why, so he did. Poor thing!"

"You like him dog?" asked John. Absently he opened a square of calico which he had tied to his belt, disclosing an odd assortment of bones, bits of fat, and odds and ends of food. To this collection he added the last scrap of the dismembered pie, folded up the cloth, tied it again to his belt, and then knelt down to examine the dog.

"Of course, I like him. He's a good dog."

"Missee Red Hair got no dog?"

"No," said Caddie slowly, her eyes filling with tears. "Nero, our dog—he's lost."

"Look. John he go 'way. John's people go 'way. John's dog no can walk. John go far, far. Him dog no can go far. You keep?"

"Yes, John," said Caddie. "I'll keep him for you. May I, Mother?" Mrs. Woodlawn nodded at her from the dining-room door. "Oh, I'll be so glad to keep him, John. I love to have a dog."

"Good," said John. He straightened himself and folded his arms.

"Look, Missee Red Hair. You keep scalp belt, too?"

"The scalp belt?" echoed Caddie uncertainly. She felt the old prickling sensation up where her scalp lock grew as she looked at the belt with its gruesome decorations of human hair.

"Him very old," said John, picking up the belt with calm familiarity. "John's father, great chief, him take many scalps. Now John no do. John have many friend. John no want scalp. You keep?" John held it out.

Gingerly, with the tips of her thumb and first finger, Caddie took it. "What shall I do with it?" she asked dubiously.

"You keep," said the Indian. "John come back in moon of yellow leaves. John go now far, far. Him might lose. You keep?"

"Yes," said Caddie, "I keep. When you come back in the moon of yellow leaves, I will have it safe for you, and your dog, too."

"Missee Red Hair good girl," said John.

He drew his blanket around him and stalked out. From the doorway Caddie watched him go. His dog limped to the door, too, and Caddie had to put her arms around his neck to keep him from following.

"Good-by, John," she called. "Have a good journey!" John was already on his pony. He raised an arm in salute and rode quickly out of the farmyard.

"Well, of all things!" cried Mrs. Woodlawn, bustling into the kitchen with a great sigh of relief. "You do have a way with savages, Caroline Augusta Woodlawn! I declare, this kitchen smells to heaven of smoky buckskin. Let's open all the windows and doors for a minute and let it out. And, for mercy's sake, Caddie, put that awful scalp belt somewhere in the barn. I couldn't sleep of nights if I knew it was hanging in my house."

Caddie took the scalp belt and the dog out to the barn. She hid the scalp belt in a safe, dry place, where she could easily get it to show to the boys. They had gone part way to Eau Galle to meet Father. Wouldn't they be green with envy when they knew what they had missed?

There was an empty box stall in the barn. In it Caddie made a nice bed of hay for John's dog. She washed his hurt foot in warm water and brought him a bowl of warm milk. Then she covered him with an old horse blanket, and sat beside him, stroking the rough head. He was an ugly dog, without Nero's silky coat and beautiful eyes, but he licked her hand gratefully, and already Caddie loved him.

"I've got a dog," she whispered to herself. "I've got a dog of my very own to keep until John comes back." And she was unaccountably happy.

So the boys found her, when they burst into the barn a few moments later.

"Ma says you've got Indian John's scalp belt! Let's see it! Let's see it!"

"All right. But no snatching. I've got to keep it nice for John when he comes back."

"Keep it *nice*," jeered Warren. "I never knew a scalp belt could be *nice*."

"Well, this one is, Master Warren," said Caddie,

displaying her treasure, "and we're going to keep it so."

Hetty and little Minnie crowded after Tom and Warren. It was a simple buckskin belt ornamented with colored beads, and from it hung three long tails of black hair, each with a bit of shriveled skin at the end.

"Ooh! ooh! ooh!" said Hetty. "Is it real hair off people's heads?"

"Sure," said Tom, lifting a lock of Hetty's hair and pretending to amputate it. "Just like this. Bing! bing! and you're a dead one."

"Ooh! ooh! Don't let him scalp me, Caddie!" wailed Hetty.

"He's just trying to tease you, Hetty. The louder you yell, the better he likes it," advised Caddie.

"It's Indians', not white folks' scalp locks anyway," said Warren. "See how black they are."

"But how about a nice long red one to surprise John when he comes back?" continued Tom. "Hetty's would look so pretty. Where's the butcher knife, Warren?"

"Help! help!" wailed Hetty. "I'll tell Father on you, so I will, and I guess he'll tan your hide for you good and proper, Tom Woodlawn."

Tom laughed. "Baby!" he said. "I wouldn't hurt you. Don't you know that? But, listen, Caddie, I've got an idea."

"Spit it out," said Caddie calmly.

"Well, look," said Tom. "All the children will want to see this scalp belt. Why don't we make some money on it?"

"Money?" echoed Caddie incredulously. "However could we make money on a scalp belt?"

"Well, maybe not exactly money. But we could charge pins or marbles or arrowheads or whatever anybody had to give us to let them take a peep. Do you see?"

"Yes," said Caddie, her face brightening. "Yes, I see—a sort of peep show! But we couldn't let them handle it, Tom. John will come back for it in the fall, and it would be terrible if it were all worn out. It belonged to his father, who was a great chief and who cut off those scalps himself. John's so proud of him."

"Hmm," said Tom. "I'm glad I've got something better than that to be proud of *my* father for. But, listen, Caddie, we won't let them touch the old thing. When you said peep show, it gave me another idea. We'll hang it up in a box with a little curtain in front of it, and after the children have paid their admissions, we'll draw back the curtain and let them take a look."

"What a bully idea!" shouted Warren.

Even Hetty forgot to look grieved and put-upon, and shouted: "Bully!"

"That's fine, Tom," said Caddie, "and maybe we can get a candle end to light it up like a real stage. You 'member the torches at the medicine show we saw in St. Louis?"

"You bet!" cried Tom, "and we'll make a sign, too. What was John's father's name, Caddie?"

"I don't know. Couldn't we just make up a name?"

"Sure," cried Warren. "How about Big Chief Sit-on-the-Fire-and-Put-It-Out?"

"Oh, that's *too* silly, Warren."

"Big Chief Red-Bird-with-a-White-Feather-in-Its-Tail," suggested Hetty.

"Too long and hard to print."

"I know!" said Tom. "Chief Bloody Tomahawk! How's that? His tomahawk must have been bloody when he got done cutting off scalps."

"Ooh! you give me the shivers, Tom," wailed Hetty.

"All right," agreed Caddie. "We'll call it Big Chief Bloody Tomahawk's favorite scalp belt."

"As if he had lots more and just tossed this one off in a jolly moment," chuckled Tom. "Let's have the show next Saturday afternoon."

"All right. Let's."

"Oh, please, may I tell?" begged Hetty.

Suddenly they all looked at her, and astonishment and delight dawned slowly over their faces. At last Hetty was going to be useful.

"Sure, Hetty!" cried Tom. "Tell everybody you see. Tell everybody in the whole country. The more children that come, the more we make. Go ahead and tell everybody."

Hetty could not believe her ears, thus to be urged to tell, when usually they set upon her and held her mouth at the very suggestion of telling anything. She looked from one to another for confirmation.

"Go ahead," said Caddie kindly. "Didn't you hear Tom say so?" They really meant it! With an exclamation of delight, Hetty raced away for her bonnet and mittens. What a lot of telling she could do before Saturday afternoon!

14 · A Dollar's Worth

The next day was Thursday. Hetty had already done
her work well. The school children crowded about
Tom and Caddie and Warren asking questions. Was it
true that they had a real Indian scalp belt? Did it
have a hundred scalps on it? Had John really given it
to Caddie to keep? What did it look like? Were there
any light-colored scalp locks on it? When could they
see it? How much would they have to pay? During the
first questions the Woodlawn children maintained a
mysterious silence. To the last two they deigned a
reply.

"You can see it on Saturday afternoon in our barn,
and you can pay a marble or a stick of candy or a

piece of flint, or anything you've got that you want
to trade to see it."

"I've got a good slingshot crotch. Will you take
that?" shouted someone.

"I've got a picture card that came from back East.
Will you take that?"

It appeared that business would be very good.

In the middle of the morning, through the sound of
droning voices chanting the reading lesson, a timid
knock was heard on the schoolhouse door. Miss Parker,
on her throne at the other end of the room, did not
hear it. It came again and the children began turning
their heads around to look at the door. First the outer
door opened and closed. There was a moment of
silence. Then the cloakroom door opened every so
softly, and an Indian woman entered the schoolroom
in her silent moccasins. She stood a moment, troubled
and ill at ease, searching the schoolroom with her
bright black eyes. A large bundle which she carried,
she rested beside the door. Caddie knew who she was.
She was Sam Hankinson's wife, the mother of the little
half-breed boys who traded lunches with the Woodlawns. Her little boys turned now and saw her, and
the youngest one held out his arms and gave a little
stifled cry. With a swift movement, like a bird alight-
ing from a low bough, the Indian woman ran to her

children and knelt beside them, gathering first one and
then another into her arms. She spoke to them in her
own language, words guttural, broken, and soft as the
chatter of a mother partridge to her brood. The boys
answered in the same language, clinging to her and
crying. By this time half of the white children were
on their feet and Miss Parker had come down from her
platform. The reading lesson was forgotten in a sudden sense of trouble and unrest.

"Ma! Ma!" cried the three little boys, clinging to the
Indian woman and sobbing. Each of them in turn
she pressed against her heart, then held each little
brown head between her hands, pushing back the
tangled hair and looking earnestly into the face as if
she would fix its image in her mind forever. When she
had done this, she kissed each one upon the forehead
and stood up. They still clung around her skirts, crying: "Ma! Ma! Don't go! Don't!"

The Indian woman put them away from her, and
stood straight and alone. The tears were running unheeded down her cheeks. To Miss Parker she said: "I
go to my people." Then she turned and left the schoolroom. At the door she took up her bundle and swung it
onto her shoulders. She did not look back. The cloakroom door closed, and then the outside door. They saw
her pass by the window, going toward the woods. For

a moment the only sound in the schoolroom was the sobbing of the three little boys.

Then Miss Parker said sharply: "Go on with your reading, please."

The drone of voices rose again. But it was as if a dark shadow or an icy wind had gone through the schoolhouse and changed everything. Caddie went on reading, but three bright tears fell on the page of her book and made odd little blisters over the type.

That evening she spoke about it to Mother.

"Why did she go away like that, Mother? She didn't want to go and leave her children, and they didn't want her to go, either."

"It is hard to explain to you, Caddie," said Mother. "You see, Mr. Hankinson married her when there were very few white people in this country. He was not ashamed of her then. But now that there are more and more of his own people coming to live here, he is ashamed that his wife should be an Indian. I daresay the massacree scare had something to do with it, too. Folks seem to hate the red men more than ever they did before. Though why they should, I can't say. Goodness knows, the massacre was only in their own minds. But Sam Hankinson hasn't a very strong character. Now if your father had married an Indian—"

"Father marry an Indian?" cried Tom. "He never would!"

"Perhaps not," said Mrs. Woodlawn, smiling a little and tossing her head, remembering how pretty she had been as a girl in Boston. "But, if he *had*, you may be sure that *he* would never have sent her off because he was ashamed of her. No, not a good man like your father!"

That night, after Caddie went to bed, she lay thinking for a long time. Hetty and Minnie were sound asleep. Presently she got up and lit the candle. On the chest of drawers stood her little trinket box. She opened it and looked inside. There was the silver dollar, safe and round and shining. She took it out and held it to the candlelight. It was really beautiful— beautiful in itself, aside from what it would buy. Then she knotted it securely into her handkerchief, and put the handkerchief into the pocket of her school apron. After that she climbed into bed and went to sleep.

At school the next morning the little Hankinsons were late. Their hair was untidy and their round faces were stern and unsmiling. They were never good at lessons, and this morning they were worse than ever. Their eyes were swollen with crying. But Miss Parker was tactful and did not ask too much of them.

Caddie's eyes kept wandering to them over her books. It was hard to keep her mind on spelling and sums, when she knew that they were sitting nearby, so quiet and so full of hurt bewilderment. Then she felt her dollar, heavy in her pocket, and she was pleased that she had saved it for so long.

After school she laid her hand on Gussie's arm. He was not nearly so big as Warren and she had a motherly desire to pat his head, but she didn't.

"Gussie," she said, "you and Pete and Sammie come with me to Dunnville store. I'm going to give you a surprise."

The three little half-breeds looked at her in aston-ishment. For a moment they were surprised out of their sorrow.

"What for?" asked Gussie suspiciously.

"Just for fun," said Caddie with a smile. "I've got a whole silver dollar to spend," and she jingled it against a marble and a bit of slate pencil in her pocket.

"Candy?" suggested little Sammie, with a sudden glitter in his eye.

"Yes, sirree," said Caddie importantly. "Come along and see."

Mr. Adams of Dunnville store was accustomed to visitors after school. The children often came in with a penny or two, or sometimes only wishful looks, to examine the glass jars in which he kept brown hoar-hound sticks or sticks of striped peppermint or winter-green lozenges. But today he was quite amazed when Caddie Woodlawn, with the air of a queen, ushered in the three little half-breeds and laid a silver dollar on the counter.

"I want to spend it all, Mr. Adams," she said, "so you'll have to tell me when I've used it up. I want some hoarhound and peppermint and some pink wintergreens, and then I want three tops in different colors with good strong strings, and will you please tell me how much that is, because if there's anything left I want to get some more things?"

"Well, upon my word!" exclaimed Mr. Adams. "And bless my soul, too! But does your mother know you're spending a silver dollar, Caddie?"

"Not yet. But it's all right. It's my own dollar and Father said I could spend it as I liked, and I'll tell Mother as soon as I get home."

The little Hankinsons looked on in amazement. The black mood of despair which had enveloped them all day had turned into wonder, and now wonder was rapidly giving way to incredulous delight. Candy! Tops! No one had ever bought such things for them before.

"Well, Miss Caddie, that comes to thirty cents," said Mr. Adams, when the bewildered boys with the help of Caddie had selected the candy and tops.

They were grinning now from ear to ear, and Caddie thought that, with so much money left to spend, she

had better be a little wise. "I'd like to see some combs now, if you please. I'd like three small ones if they aren't too dear."

"Here you are, my girl," said the storekeeper, bringing down a dusty box from a shelf. He was smiling, too, by now, and almost as eager as the little Hankinsons to see what Caddie would buy next.

"I think," said Caddie, presenting the three combs, "that your mama would like you to keep your hair combed nice and tidy, and it'll be more fun if you've got combs of your own."

Unused to gifts of any sort, the small brown boys beamed as delightedly over combs as over tops and candy. Caddie looked inquiringly at Mr. Adams.

"It's not gone yet," he said encouragingly. "You've still got thirty cents."

Caddie examined her protégés with maternal eyes. Certainly their noses needed attention as well as their hair.

"I guess handkerchiefs had better come next," she said thoughtfully. "Thirty cents' worth of nice, cheerful, red handkerchiefs, if you please."

Mr. Adams had the very thing, large enough to meet any emergency, and of a fine turkey red. Caddie was satisfied, and the little Hankinsons were speechless with delight. The red was like music to their half-savage eyes. They waved the handkerchiefs in the air. They capered about and jostled each other and laughed aloud as Caddie had never heard them do before.

"Now you can go home," said Caddie, giving each of them a friendly pat, "and have a good time, and mind you remember to have clean noses and tidy hair on Monday when you come to school."

Dazed with their good fortune, they tumbled out of the store, whooping with joy and entirely forgetting (if they ever knew) that thanks were in order. Caddie and the storekeeper watched them race away, the red handkerchiefs flapping joyously in the breeze.

"Well, young lady," said Mr. Adams with an amused twinkle in his eye, "now your dollar's gone, and you didn't get a thing out of it for yourself."

"Oh, yes, I did, Mr. Adams!" she cried, and then she stopped. It was no use trying to tell a grownup. It was hard even to explain to herself. And yet she'd had her dollar's worth.

She found more words for it later when Tom, feeling himself for once the thrifty one, protested.

"But Caddie, you needn't have spent your whole dollar. You could have got them each a top or a hoarhound stick, and kept the rest for yourself."

"No, Tom, it had to be all of it. I wanted to drive that awful lonesome look out of their eyes, and it did, Tom. It did!"

15 · "Fol de Rol-lol"

On Saturday afternoon, Mrs. Woodlawn looked out of the window and cried: "Great sakes! Whatever has happened? Don't tell me there's another massacre scare!" Clara ran to the window and looked out, too. A whole procession of children was straggling up the road and into the farmyard.

Clara began to laugh.

"Oh, Mother," she said, "it's only the scalp belt. Caddie and Tom are exhibiting it this afternoon."

Indeed, Tom and Caddie were busy at that very moment taking admissions at the barn door. Inside the barn Warren and Hetty were seating the guests on barrels and boxes or old wagon seats and trying to maintain order. Little Minnie stood at one side with her finger in her mouth, too overwhelmed to speak. It was an important occasion.

Fastened up against the harness rack was a box with a calico curtain strung across it. Here was the "show" and all eyes fixed themselves upon it. A sign in straggling letters on a piece of board assured the audience that these were the "favorite scalps of Bloody Tomahawk."

At last, after the audience had begun to shuffle its feet and utter impatient "me-ows," Tom came forward with the fine assurance of an old showman.

"Ladies and gents," he said, "you are now about to see one of the seven wonders of Dunnville. I don't know what the other six are, but anyway, I guess you'll agree that this is the best of the lot. Curtain, please! Light, please!"

Hetty and Warren struggled with the complicated strings of the small curtain. Caddie held up a candle stub and one of Mother's precious sulphur matches. There was a scratch, a spurt of blue flame, a strong odor of sulphur, and then the interior of the box was flooded with candlelight. The audience pressed forward to gaze in awe at the three tails of black hair, which had once adorned the heads of three unfortunate savages.

"The one and only," intoned Tom, who was now in

his element, "the favorite and best scalp belt of that ferocious chief, Bloody Tomahawk. He scalped Indians, he slew a thousand buffalo, he burned down white men's houses and barns—"

"Faith, Tom Woodlawn, and ye'll do the same," cried an indignant voice. "Wurra-wurra! Do ye not know better than to light a candle in yer father's barn?" Robert Ireton stood in the barn door, his good-natured face as stormy as a thunder cloud. Caddie hastened to snuff the candle.

"Oh, Robert," she said, "we've done no harm. We're only having a show. Look! I've put out the candle and the barn's not burned down, either. Please, Robert, get your banjo and sing us a song. It will be a part of the show."

"Please, Robert, do," begged all the children, for Robert's fame as a musician had gone all through the neighborhood. Robert never had to be coaxed to sing. A smile broke through the clouds of disapproval on his face. In a moment he had fetched his banjo and seated himself in their midst.

There was another moment of delightful suspense as he tuned the instrument and twanged a few preliminary chords.

"Sing 'Paddy's Leather Breeches,'" cried Tom, who was glad to give up the center of the stage when the next performer was Robert.

"Yes, yes! 'Paddy's Leather Breeches,' " shouted the children.

"Faith, then! 'Paddy's Leather Breeches' it shall be," said Robert, "but, mind, you must all join in on the 'fol de rol-lols.' "

"We will! we will!" shouted the children. Twang! twang! twang! went the banjo.

> *"On the road to Clonmel* [sang Robert],
> *At the Sign of the Bell,*
> *Paddy Haggerty kept a nate shanty.*
> *He kept mate, figs, an' bread*
> *An' a nate lodgin' bed.*
> *Well liked for the country he lived in.*
> *Sing fol de rol-lol.*
> *Sing fol de rol-lol.*
> *Sing fol de rol-lol, de rol lido!"*

A swelling chorus of voices flung the "fol de rol-lols" as high as the rafters.

> *"One night the snow fallin' down*
> *He could not get to town*
> *An' Paddy was ate out completely."*

Here something always seemed to be left out or added on to spoil the meter, but Robert twanged on as gayly as ever, fitting his music to the words as he knew them with never a care for rhyme or reason.

"*That night as he lay dreaming of fairies and witches,*
He heard an uproar
Outside of his door
And he jumped up to strail on his breeches."

"Sing fol de rol-lol," shouted the children.

"*The words were scarce spoke*
When the door came unbroke
And they gathered 'round Paddy like leeches.
Sayin', 'By the Big Matchel Gob
If ye don't give us grub
We'll ate ye clean out o' your breeches!' "

"Sing fol de rol-lol! Sing fol de rol-lol!"

" '*Sure, they've got to be fed!'*
He slipped up to the bed
Which held Judy his own darlin' wife in,
An' 'twas there they agreed
How to give 'em a feed,
So he stepped out an' brought a big knife in.
Sing fol de rol-lol.
Sing fol de rol-lol.
Sing fol de rol-lol, de rol lido!

"They cut up the waist
 Of the breeches the best
 And they ripped off the buttons and stitches.
 They cut 'em in strips,
 By the way they was striped,
 An' they boiled up the old leather breeches."

"Sing fol de rol-lol!" roared the audience. "Fol de rol-lol, de rol lido!"

"When it was stewed
 An' on a dish strewed,
 The boys cried out, 'Lord be thankit!'
 But 'twas little they knew
 That 'twas leather-be-goo
 B'iled out o' Paddy's old breeches.
 Sing fol de rol-lol.
 Sing fol de rol-lol.

"As they messed on the stuff,
 Says Andy, ' 'Tis tough.'
 Says Paddy, 'Ye're no judge o' mutton.'
 Then Brian McQuirk,
 On the p'int of his fork,
 Held up a large ivory button.
 Sing fol de rol-lol.
 Sing fol de rol-lol.
 Sing fol de rol-lol, de rol lido!

> *"'They've p'isoned the feast*
> *Let's send for a priest!'*
> *They jumps on their legs an' they screeches,*
> *An' from that very night*
> *They'd knock out yer daylight*
> *If ye'd mention the old leather breeches."*

Such a joyous howl of "fol de rol-lols" marked the
end of the song as set the horses to jumping and paw-
ing in their stalls and John's dog to barking like a mad
thing. And so ended in music the show which had
begun with scalp locks.

On counting up the gate receipts, the Woodlawn
children discovered that they had a tidy collection of
marbles, old birds' nests, butternuts, pins with colored
heads, slingshot crotches, and various other objects of
interest or art.

"I guess we did pretty well," said Caddie pleasantly
as she divided the spoils.

But Tom pocketed his share in silence. Some dis-
turbing thought seemed to have occurred to him.
"Katie Hyman didn't come to the show," he said. "I
guess she's about the only one who didn't."

"What do you expect?" demanded Caddie with a
little touch of scorn in her voice. "She'd be scared to
death of a scalp belt."

"She hasn't been to school since the massacree scare," volunteered Hetty.

"I know it," said Tom.

Caddie stopped to think. "No, she hasn't," she said slowly. She had thought so much about John and the little Hankinsons that Katie had never entered her head. Now a series of vivid pictures flashed across her mind. Katie standing in the barn, her eyes wide with fear, her hands pressed to her breast, saying, "Cross my heart"; Katie fainting when Caddie returned from her wild ride; Katie pale and silent the next day, starting for home, holding her mother's hand; and last of all Katie's place on the bench in the corner of the schoolroom, *empty!* "I wonder," said Caddie.

"Maybe she's sick," said Tom, trying to seem careless about it.

"Maybe she is," said Caddie, "and, if she is, I guess it's my fault. We'd better go and see her."

They ran to the house for permission.

"Yes, do go," said Mrs. Woodlawn. "I've worried about the poor little thing myself. Here, take her some of these molasses cookies, and see that you get back before dark."

"Couldn't we take the scalp belt to show her, Caddie?" inquired Tom.

"I'll let you," said Caddie, "but she won't like it."

"Aw, golly! I bet she would. She's the only one who hasn't seen it. I'd hate to be the only one who hadn't seen it, wouldn't you?"

Caddie wrapped up the scalp belt in a piece of brown paper, and away they went.

"You go up to the door and knock, Caddie," said Tom when they reached the little log house where Katie and her mother lived. "I just came along to keep you company, you know."

Caddie went up and knocked, and Mrs. Hyman let them in.

"Yes, Katie's been very poorly ever since the scare," said her mother. "But do come in. I think the sight of you will do her good."

Katie sat up in bed, a little knitted shawl about her shoulders and pillows piled behind her. Her face was so pale, her eyes so blue, her hair so golden—like a little girl in a dream or a fairy tale. On the rough wall beside her was pinned the finest Valentine from Dunnville store. Tom looked at it and suddenly lost his voice.

"I'm sorry you've been poorly," said Caddie, coming up to the bed.

Katie reached out her little thin hand and caught Caddie's sturdy one. "Oh, Caddie," she said, "I want to feel if you are real. You look so real! I'm glad you

came. I've had such nightmares since the scare. In them people are always hunting for you, and I'm the only one who knows that you are away being scalped by the Indians, and I can't tell because I've crossed my heart. Oh, you can't know how awful it is!"

Caddie sat down on the edge of the bed, awkwardly holding the little hand in hers. "I shouldn't have made you cross your heart," she said. "It was real unkind of me, Katie. But I didn't mean it that way. You see, just then, I was more scared of the white folks than the Indians. Katie, honestly, you mustn't be afraid of the Indians. Most of them are just as good and friendly as can be. Let me tell you about John and what he gave me to keep for him before he went away."

Tom drew up a chair and together they told her

about John's departure and the scalp belt show, and
how Mrs. Hankinson had gone away, and what Caddie
had done with her silver dollar. Encouraged by the
little shadowy smiles about her lips, they piled on all
the lively details they could remember or invent, and,
before they were through, Katie was laughing and
there was a little pinkness in each pale cheek.

"Oh, I should have liked to see them with their
bright red handkerchiefs!" she said. "I—I *almost* wish
I could have seen the scalp belt show."

"Well," said Tom, "it's here," and he tapped the
brown paper parcel which lay on his knee.

"Here?" echoed Katie, looking a little startled.

"Yes," said Tom. "Caddie thought you'd be afraid
to look at it. But I knew you wouldn't want to be the
only one who hadn't seen it."

"She doesn't want to see it, Tom. It's only a bunch
of old Indian scalps," said Caddie, fearing that all
their cheerful talk would have been wasted if Katie
were obliged to see the gruesome object. But Katie sat
up straighter in her pillows. There was a kind of reso-
lute bravery about her that no one had ever noticed
there before.

"I *do* want to see it—very much."

Tom unwrapped the brown paper and held up the
belt. "Isn't that a beauty?" he demanded.

Katie gasped. "Yes," she said. "Yes—it—is—a beauty." She even touched one of the tails of hair, and when she had, she looked quite proud and pleased.

"Do wrap it up now, Tom," said Caddie, "and here are some cookies Mother sent which you'll find much nicer than scalps. I hope you'll be well soon, and now we must go."

"Thank you for coming," said Katie. "I think I *will* be well soon." And, indeed, she did look better already.

As they rose to go Tom's eye rested again on the "rose is red" Valentine. Katie looked at it, too. Then their eyes met in some embarrassment.

"Tom," said Katie, "I guessed who sent it."

Tom laughed. "You did? That was pretty smart of you, Katie."

All the way home Tom whistled and sang: "Fol de rol-lol, fol de rol-lol, fol de rol-lol, de rol lido!"

16 · *Warren Performs*

Now the air began to be warm and the sun to shine. One day, when the three adventurers were in the woods hunting for arbutus to take to Teacher, they heard a roaring on the river.

"The ice is going out," said Tom. "Let's go and see." They ran to the river bank and stood together, watching. They could not hear each other speak above the sound of grinding, crashing ice. By evening the ice had piled itself in places as high as the tavern at Dunnville. The tavern on the other side of the river was cut off from the town entirely. In summer a ferry plied between the two banks, in winter folks crossed on the ice, but now the two banks were separated by a great jam of ice that groaned and creaked and made its slow way down to larger rivers.

"It won't be long now until the Little Steamer comes again," said Mrs. Woodlawn with a smile. "Of course we shouldn't complain now that they bring some of our mail in on sledges, but, just the same, I like it better to be in touch with Boston and the rest of the world. Children, what should you think of having your cousin Annabelle from Boston here to visit you this summer? Her parents have been talking of letting her make the journey for some time. She could go by the steam cars to St. Louis, visit Uncle Edmund's folks, and come on here by boat. I think I'll sit down and write them this very day."

"What's she like, Mother?"

"Oh, I haven't seen her for years, of course, but she was a darling little girl and very accomplished. She's not so old as Clara—nearer Caddie's age, I believe, but, well—she's been reared as a lady, and will be nicely finished, I am sure."

"Oh! That kind of girl!" said Tom.

Caddie's heart, which had undergone a certain disagreeable chill at Mother's, "but, well—*she's* been reared as a lady," warmed pleasantly again at the deep scorn in Tom's voice. Tom was more than a brother, he was a friend.

However, the whole family looked with interest and a sense of expectation at the letter which Mother wrote and directed to Miss Annabelle Grey of Boston. It stood upon a shelf in the parlor for many days, waiting for the Little Steamer to come and take it.

Before the ice went out, Father and Robert Ireton had gone through the woods adjoining the farm and tapped the sugar maple trees. This was a delightful business to Tom, Caddie, and Warren, who made the rounds of the sap buckets in the afternoons after school, and felt that they were chiefly responsible for the maple syrup that was so good on Mrs. Conroy's hot cakes.

And now vacation loomed delightfully ahead. The winter term of school was almost over and Miss Parker would go and teach the children of Durand their A B Cs and multiplication tables for three months. The last day of school was to be a "speaking" day with songs by the school and recitations by some of the pupils. Caddie and Warren both had pieces. Caddie's was a very noble one beginning:

> *"A traveller on a dusty road*
> *Strewed acorns on the lea,*
> *And one took root and sprouted up*
> *And grew into a tree."*

The poem went on to say that, as carelessly tossed acorns may grow into great oaks, so may little words and deeds of kindness grow into great and beautiful things. Under Mother's coaching Caddie had practiced it with gestures and a fine Boston accent, and it was quite perfect.

But everyone felt a little doubtful of Warren. His piece was so short that it seemed impossible that he should be able to forget it or mix it up in any way. But Warren was not gifted as a public speaker. He said it over and over as he went about the house.

> *"If at first you don't succeed,*
> *Try, try again!*

That's easy, isn't it? You don't think I'll forget it, do you?"

"Of course not, Warren," said Caddie. "Just don't get stage fright, that's all."

"What's stage fright?" asked Warren in a worried tone.

"Oh, just being scared when you have to get up and see so many eyes looking at you."

"You won't have time to get scared with a piece as short as that," laughed Tom. Then he struck a dramatic attitude and declaimed:

> *"If at first you don't fricassee,*
> *Fry, fry a hen!"*

This struck Warren as tremendously funny, and he went about the house giving Tom's version of the piece as often as he gave the correct one.

On the morning of the "speaking" day the sky was full of black clouds. There was a heavy stillness in the air with an occasional drop of rain and a rumbling of distant thunder.

"There's going to be a dreadful storm," said Mrs. Woodlawn. "I can feel it in the air. I planned to take Minnie and baby Joe to the speaking, but I don't dare risk it on such a day. It looks black enough for a tornado or a cloudburst. I really believe that you children had all better stay at home where you'll be safe."

"Stay at home from the speaking?" cried Caddie in dismay, thinking of her best white apron so nicely starched, and of the gestures and the Boston accent. Were they all to be wasted?

"Why, Ma—I mean Mother, we've gone to school in stormy weather all winter," said Tom. "It won't hurt us."

"I think Mother's right. We better stay at home," said Warren, who was beginning to look a little pale around the gills. Ever since he had arisen that morning the air about him had been filled with muttered "try,

try again"s, and sometimes with "fry, fry a hen"s, which slipped out inadvertently.

"*I'm* going," said Hetty stoutly.

"Well, well, go along," said Mrs. Woodlawn, "but I'll keep the little ones at home."

So away the four Woodlawns trudged to school.

The schoolroom was decorated with evergreen branches and a loop of faded bunting, and the children were conspicuously starched and clean. Miss Parker herself had on a shiny black silk apron instead of the usual one of speckled calico. A few of the Dunnville parents sat on benches at the front of the room, looking self-conscious and important. Caddie's heart beat a little faster, but not so much for herself as for Warren, whose face wore a look of dark foreboding. Could one possibly forget a piece so short as his? wondered Caddie uncomfortably. Then she heard Miss Parker calling her name, and she got up without any hesitation, mounted the platform, and made the neat curtsy Mother had taught her.

> "*A traveller on a dusty road*
> *Strewed acorns on the lea,*
> *And one took root . . .*"

It went off perfectly, gestures, Boston accent and everything.

She dropped another curtsy and returned to her seat, feeling that, perhaps for the first time in her life, she had acquitted herself exactly as an "accomplished" young lady would have done. Too bad that Mother had not been there to see! While she was still glowing with this novel achievement, she heard Miss Parker announce:

"And now Master Warren Woodlawn will be heard in a recitation. Come right up here in front, Warren."

For a moment Warren clung desperately to the bench on which he sat. Then with a rush he mounted the platform and began to recite in a very loud voice.

> *"If at first you don't fricassee,*
> *Fry, fry a hen!"*

"Oh!" said Caddie.

"Oh!" said everybody else in various degrees of consternation and amusement. The titters spread into a roar of laughter.

"Warren Woodlawn," said Miss Parker grimly, "you will please stop and see me after school." She rapped on her desk with her ruler, and silence was restored. But what a merry silence—for everyone except Warren, and poor, outraged Miss Parker.

The "whoop" and "hurrah!" with which school always let out for the term was somewhat spoiled for Tom and Caddie and Hetty. How could one jump and shout with Warren still sitting uncomfortably on his bench waiting for Miss Parker to finish shaking hands with the parents? Besides, the storm which had been saving its fury all the morning was just beginning to break over the schoolhouse. There were gusts of wind and rain and clap after clap of thunder with jagged streaks of lightning in the dark sky. The children scattered for their homes more quickly and silently than usual. Tom, Caddie, and Hetty stayed in the cloakroom waiting for Warren.

"Golly! I wish she'd hurry up," said Tom. "We're going to get a good ducking before we get home if she doesn't."

"Let's go in," said Caddie. Cautiously they pushed the schoolroom door and entered the room which was now deserted except for Warren and Miss Parker.

"Now, Warren," Miss Parker was saying, "I give you one more opportunity to say your piece correctly. Now go ahead, do." Warren, his face very red, his hands very much in the way, began to mumble the famous piece. But all that would come out, try as he might, was "Fry, fry a hen." Ominously Miss Parker reached for her ruler.

"Oh, say, ma'am," said Tom, coming quickly forward with his nicest smile, "I guess it's my fault, 'cause I taught him that. You see, it's the first piece he ever spoke and I guess he's pretty scared. I hope you'll forgive him and lay the blame on me."

Miss Parker laid down her ruler with a sigh of relief. "Well, well," she said, "it's the last day of school. Run along now, all of you."

But as they were starting home, all happily reunited, she ran after them to say: "Better come back and wait until the storm's over. You've got a long ways to go."

"We can make it," called back Tom cheerfully. "Mother'll worry if we're late. Good-by, Miss Parker."

"Good-by! Good-by! Good-by!" called the other three.

"Good-by!" called Miss Parker, "and you're nice children, all of you, even if Warren did disgrace me."

Before they had gone half a mile, the storm broke with all its strength. Lightning and thunder crashed and flashed together in a perfect fury! Stunned by the force of it, the children ran for shelter under the great oak tree that marked the halfway point between home and school. Its branches lashed and creaked, but it was something sturdy to cling to. Caddie and Warren and Hetty clung together under the tree, but Tom urged them on.

"Let's get home," he shouted, "let's run for it."

"Oh, please let's wait here," begged the others.

"No!" cried Tom, "we've got to get home. Come along, every one of you." When Tom made up his mind, the others followed him. Shielding their faces, they dashed out of shelter and along the road.

Crash! Bang! There was a blinding flash and something hurled them onto the ground. Dazed and crying, they picked themselves up and looked back. The oak tree had been split in two by lightning. Another moment under its shelter and all of them might have been killed.

How they ran that last half mile! No one had ever run it so quickly before. Even Hetty could not outstrip the others to be the first to tell. Breathless and wild-eyed, with wet and muddy clothes, they rushed into the kitchen.

"*Mother!*" they shouted all together. "Mother, listen to what happened to us!"

17 · Pee-Wee

Some days later the members of the Woodlawn family were finishing breakfast. Caddie, Tom, and Warren, at one side of the table, were buzzing and tittering over some project for the day. Now that school was over, their days were full of delight. Today they were talking of going to Chimney Bluffs. Father folded his napkin and pushed back his chair.

"All play and no work," said Father, purposely misquoting the old adage, "makes Tom, Caddie, and Warren lazy children. Isn't that so?" He looked down the table at them and smiled.

"Oh, no, Father," said Caddie, "we've been very industrious."

"The results of their industry," said Mrs. Woodlawn dryly, "being dirty faces, holes in their stockings,
and three-cornered rents in trousers and pettitcoats."

"Well," said Father, "suppose I put them to work?
I'm going to give you three children the far field to
plow, the one next to the woods. You may hitch Betsy
to the plow and take turns at it if you wish. Take as
long as you like, but I'll expect your task well done."

"All by ourselves? Without Robert? That'll be bully!
We can go to Chimney Bluffs some other day," cried
the three adventurers, and away they dashed for
Betsy and the plow. Indian John's dog barked and ran
with them. It was almost as good as having Nero.

The first few furrows were great fun. Sometimes in
the past they had turned up Indian arrowheads in
plowing the far field, but nothing so fortunate happened today and plowing gets very monotonous after
a while. It was a sparkling spring day with a blue sky
and a warm sun. The silver birches in the wood had
begun to glow with a faint aura of budding green, and
the willows at the edge of the river were turning
yellow. Overhead flew a phœbe bird, crying: "Pee-
wee! Pee-wee!"

"Let's take turns with the plow," said Tom. "All
three of us don't have to go around every time. It takes
only one to guide the plow. Let one guide the plow

twice around the field while the other two sit in the fence corner and tell stories."

"Hurrah!" yelled Warren. "I speak to be first to sit in the fence corner."

"All right," said Tom. "I'll take Betsy around first while you and Caddie sit. I'll be thinki _ up a story."

"You spoke to be first to sit," said Caddie to Warren. "I speak to be the one to sit when Tom tells his story."

"Oh, that's no fair. Tom's got to tell it to me, too."

"All right," said Tom again. "I'll tell it twice, but first I've got to make it up." He flapped the reins over Betsy's back, caught the handles of the plow, and started his first furrow. Caddie and Warren settled down in a sunny corner of the zigzag rail fence to think up stories. They usually retold Robert Ireton's lusty Irish tales or some old favorites from the tattered volume of Andersen's *Fairy Tales*. Sometimes they even told the stories which Mother read them from *The Young Ladies' Friend* or *The Mother's Assistant*, when they weren't too dull or moral. But Tom made his stories up. That's why Tom's stories were always in demand. Tom's stories had the virtue of novelty, and they were full of wild and bloody action. That they, too, were a sort of compound of Ireton and Andersen did not occur to the children, who knew few stories, except those in the Bible and the school reader.

"Have you thought it up yet?" cried Warren and Caddie, as Tom came around at the end of his first furrow. "Pee-wee! Pee-wee!" called the phœbe bird overhead. Betsy would have stopped, but Tom slapped the reins over her back and swung into his second furrow.

"Yep!" he called back. "I'm gettin' it."

Reluctantly Warren took the plow when Tom came back from his second round. Caddie and John's dog cuddled close to Tom as he sat down. The spring air was still a little keen for sitting long in comfort.

"Well, begin," said Caddie.

Tom's eyes were bright with satisfaction over his

story. "Well," he said, "once upon a time there was an old farmer named Pee-Wee."

"What a funny name for a farmer!" exclaimed Caddie.

"Never you mind that," said Tom, a trifle impatient at being interrupted. "You'll know why his name had to be Pee-Wee in a minute, if you'll listen."

"Go on, then."

"Well, once there was an old farmer named Pee-Wee, and he had a farm beside a lake. And one day he was out plowing up his field when a little bird flew overhead, calling 'Pee-wee! Pee-wee!' Now, old man Pee-Wee had a pretty bad temper, and he thought the little bird was just making fun of him. So what did he do but pick up a rock he had just plowed out, and heave it at the bird. 'I'll teach you to make fun of old man Pee-Wee!' says he. The bird just flapped his wings and flew on, but the rock fell back and hit one of Pee-Wee's oxen on the head, and it fell over dead.

"Well, old man Pee-Wee was mighty mad, but he wouldn't ever let anything get him down. So he stopped plowing and skinned his ox and took the hide to town to see what he could get for it.

"Well, just as he was driving into town, he saw a secondhand store with a lot of old furniture sitting out in front, and there were some young people running about and playing I Spy. Just as Pee-Wee drove up, he saw a very rich young man run and hide himself in a big, empty churn, and pull the cover shut after him. So Pee-Wee got down off his wagon and took the ox hide in to the storekeeper.

" 'What'll you give me for this hide?' says he to the storekeeper.

" 'Why, nothing,' says the storekeeper. 'I haven't got money to spend on old ox hides.'

" 'I'll tell you what,' says Pee-Wee. "Trade me that worthless old churn for my hide, an' you'll be getting the best of the bargain.'

" 'All right,' says the storekeeper, 'if you'll carry it off.' So Pee-Wee left his hide and loaded the churn up onto his wagon.

"Now, when Pee-Wee had got the churn a little ways out into the country, the rich young man began to pound on the side of it and yell: 'Let me out! Let me out!'

" 'How so?' says Pee-Wee. 'I bought this churn and everything in it. You belong to me.'

" 'I'm rich,' says the young man. 'I'll pay you anything. Only let me out.'

"So Pee-Wee let the young man out an' the young man gave him a purse full of gold. When Pee-Wee got home, he showed all his neighbors the purse full of gold which he had got in exchange for the ox hide. As soon as they saw it, the neighbors all ran to kill their best oxen and take the hides to town. When they found they could get nothing for them, they were so mad at Pee-Wee they swore they'd never speak to him again."

"Is that all?" asked Caddie eagerly, as Tom paused for breath.

"Oh, no," said Tom, "the best part's coming."

Warren, going by on his first furrow, looked at them wistfully, but Tom motioned him on.

"Well, some time after that," continued Tom, "Pee-Wee and his old wife were out hoeing potatoes, when that same bird flew over the potato patch, and sang: 'Pee-wee! Pee-wee!'

" 'You'll try that again, will you?' yells Pee-Wee, flying into a passion. 'I'll teach you!' and he threw his hoe at the bird. But the bird flew away and the hoe came down and hit Pee-Wee's wife over the head and killed her."

"Oh, dear!" said Caddie. "Did you really mean it to kill her, Tom?"

"That's all right," said Tom, "it's just a story. So then, when Pee-Wee saw that his wife was dead, of course he felt very sorry, but he wouldn't ever let anything get him down. So he tied her sunbonnet on her to shade her face, and set her up on a seat with her back

to the lake and facing the highway which ran along by the lake at that place. Then he set a basket of oranges on one side of her and a basket of lemons on the other, and then he went and hid himself in the bushes near by. Pretty soon along came a man driving a coach and four black horses. When the man saw Pee-Wee's wife sitting beside the road, he stopped his horses and got down off the coach.

" 'Say, old lady, how do you sell your oranges?' he asked.

"Pee-Wee's wife didn't answer.

" 'How do you sell your lemons?' No answer.

"The man thought she was deaf, and he began to

shout as loud as he could: "Say, old lady, *how do you sell your oranges? How do you sell your lemons?*" Still no answer, and was he mad! Before he knew what he was doing, he reached out and gave her a punch, and the poor old woman fell over backward into the lake.

"Now Pee-Wee came out of the bushes, and he says, says he: 'You've drowned my poor old wife, you rascal. I'll have the law on you.'

" 'Oh, please, sir,' says the driver of the coach, 'don't do that. I didn't mean to drown her at all, at all. Here, I'll give you my coach and four black horses, if you'll say nothing more about it.'

" 'Very well,' says Pee-Wee, 'but see you don't go around pushing any more old women into lakes.'

"Well, Pee-Wee's neighbors had said they'd never speak to him again, but when they saw him driving a fine coach and four prancing black horses, they couldn't help coming to ask him about them. Pee-Wee told them he'd accidentally killed his wife, and how he'd set her up by the roadside, and the coachman had given him the coach and four in exchange for her. So all of the farmers knocked their old wives on the head and set them up by the road to wait for a coach."

"Good land, Tom!" cried Caddie. "They'd never do *that!*"

"Say, who's telling this story anyway?" demanded Tom irritably.

"Well, go on."

"Of course, the coach didn't come along," continued Tom, "and the other farmers were good and mad, as you may well believe."

"I should think so!" said Caddie.

"They began to plot how they could get rid of Pee-Wee. So they came to his farm one day and got him and put him in a big hogshead barrel. They headed it up with Pee-Wee inside, and they trundled it down to the lake, where they meant to drown him. Now, on the edge of the lake, there was a tavern like the one down to Dunnville, and before they drowned Pee-Wee, the farmers decided they'd go in an' get a drink to celbrate getting rid of him. So in they went, leaving Pee-Wee in the hogshead on the edge of the lake.

" 'Let me out! Let me out!' shouts Pee-Wee, pounding his fists on the sides of the hogshead.

"Now just at this time along comes an old shepherd, driving his flock of sheep. He was old and he had come a long way, an' he was mighty tired of life. So he asked Pee-Wee what was the matter, and, when Pee-Wee told him, he says, 'I'll change places with you, Pee-Wee. I'm old, I am, and mighty tired of life.' So he took the head off the barrel and let Pee-Wee out, and he got in himself. Well, Pee-Wee headed up the hogshead and went off, driving all the sheep before him to his own farm.

"Pretty soon out came the other farmers, feeling pretty gay. 'Good-by, Pee-Wee,' says they. 'Good riddance to bad rubbish,' and they up and pushed the hogshead into the lake. On their way home, they stopped by Pee-Wee's farm to divide up his things among themselves, an' there was old Pee-Wee himself with a fine new flock of sheep.

" 'How come you're here, an' where did you get those sheep?' asked the farmers. 'We thought you were at the bottom of the lake.'

" 'So I was,' says Pee-Wee. 'You put me there yourselves, didn't you? But 'tis a grand place at the bottom of the lake an' full o' sheep. I took only the smallest part for myself. There's flocks and flocks left for the rest of you.'

" 'Do tell!' says the rest of the farmers, and they were all so greedy that they ran and jumped in the lake to get flocks of sheep. Of course they never came back again, and Pee-Wee was lord and master of all their lands and cattle, and that's the end."

Caddie heaved a deep sigh.

"That's a good story, Tom," she said admiringly, "only I hope he didn't live happily every afterward."

"Well, sometimes he used to have nightmares," conceded Tom.

"My turn now," said Warren, coming up from the second round.

Caddie set her hands to the handles of the plow and chirped to Betsy. As she went away down the field, she heard Tom beginning: "Once upon a time there was an old farmer named Pee-Wee—" How many times she was to hear it again! For that became the Woodlawn children's favorite story. Many years later Caddie, herself, laughing and protesting, had to tell it over and over to begging children and grandchildren.

18 · News from the Outside

One spring day a hoarse whistle sounded down the river. "The Little Steamer!" everybody cried. "The Little Steamer is back again!"

Father hitched up the wagon and the children all clambered in behind. Mother came out with her hands full of letters for Boston. On top was the one addressed to Miss Annabelle Grey.

"If the sugar and coffee have come in, Johnny, be sure to lay in a supply."

"Yes, Harriet."

"And don't forget the mail."

"Oh, no, we won't forget the mail!" shouted everybody.

Only a few letters and papers got through by sledge

during the winter, and the first steamer in the spring was sure to be loaded with news from the outside world. The Little Steamer was a keel boat belonging to the lumber company and it was principally used to take men and goods up and down the river to different lumber camps. But for the settlers it meant something far more than this—it was the one thing that linked them up with the outside world.

The river bank was crowded with people to see the Little Steamer come in. Father drove up just as it reached the dock, and the children stood up in the back of the wagon and waved and cheered.

"What's the news, Skipper?" shouted someone on the bank. The captain tossed a coil of rope to the many eager hands on shore waiting to pull it in.

"General Lee has surrendered," he shouted back.

"Lee surrendered? No! Can it be possible? *Lee surrendered!* Then, by golly, the war is ended! The abolitionists have won the war! Hooray! Hooray!" The people on the banks began tossing up their hats and shouting.

The Woodlawn children shouted, too. "Hooray! Hooray! Hooray!"—until their throats were hoarse.

Hetty plucked Caddie by the skirt. "Why is the war over, Caddie?"

"Well, you see," said Caddie, giving Hetty an excited hug, "General Lee is the leader of the South, and when he surrenders, that means that our side and President Lincoln's side has won the war."

"Hooray!" shouted Hetty. "Hooray!"

"Hooray for the slaves! Hooray for Abraham Lincoln!" shouted Tom. The name of the president caught the crowd's fancy.

"Hooray for Honest Abe!" they cried. "Long live Abe Lincoln!"

After the excitement of this news, even the piles of letters and papers from Boston for Mother were an anticlimax. But still there was the fun of breaking the news at home to Mother and Clara and Mrs. Conroy and the men. Father almost forgot the sugar and coffee in the excitement of politics, and Hetty had to remind him. But at last they were on their way homeward, chattering and bouncing, and shouting to make their voices heard above the rattling of the wheels.

What a day it was! There were so many letters to be read, so many of the world's doings to be caught up with. That night as they sat about the fire, even nuts and candle lighters were forgotten. They sat with wide eyes and clasped hands while Mother read aloud from the back numbers of *The Young Ladies' Friend* and *The Mother's Assistant*, and Clara turned the pages of *Godey's Lady's Book* and sighed over the

beautiful costumes. At bedtime, they knelt together as
they did when the circuit rider came, and Father gave
thanks for the end of the war and begged that Mr.
Lincoln be made strong and wise to lead them back to
peace and security.

Spring came quickly in the next few days, and what
a happy spring it was, with no shadow of war to spoil
its glitter! All through the woods sprang up a carpet
of trilliums and wind flowers and hepaticas. They were
delicate pink and blue and white, and there were so
many of them that picking did not spoil them. The
wild cherry trees put on dresses of white like brides or
young ladies at their first ball. The tender new leaves
on the trees were almost as many-colored as in autumn.
Some were softly yellow, some pinkish-red, some like
bronze or copper. Later they would all be green, and
they would grow dusty with summer and look tired
and languid in the heat. But now everything was fresh
and young.

"A magic time of year," Caddie called it to herself.
She loved both spring and fall. At the turning of the
year things seemed to stir in her that were lost sight
of in the commonplace stretches of winter and
summer.

One April afternoon she went by herself to gather
flowers in the woods. The mourning doves had come
back and they were making a little sad refrain

through the singing of the pines. The buckets hung empty on the sugar maple trees, for the syrup season was ended. There were some new pine slashings that filled the air with perfume. Like the birch smoke and the smell of clover, the pine smell was a Wisconsin smell, and because she loved them so, they were a part of Caddie Woodlawn.

There was a flash of red in the branches above her head, and Caddie caught her breath in sharply. The cardinals were back! Almost every year a pair of them nested in the woods, and Father always expressed his surprise at seeing them so far north.

"They've come from the South," said Caddie to herself. "Maybe they saw Nero."

With her hands full of flowers, she skirted around the farm through the woods until she came to the hill north of the house. There she could look down and see house and barnyard spread out beneath her, and Robert Ireton spading the garden and never guessing that someone watched him from the hill. Here in the edge of the woods on the north hill was little Mary's grave. Father had made a little white picket fence around it, to show that this was no longer woods but belonged to little Mary. It was hard to remember little Mary now. She had come with them from Boston, but she had died so soon and gone to rest on the north hill. No one missed her now, and it was hard to imagine that she would have been near Hetty's age, if she had lived. But sometimes it was nice to come here and sit beside her, because it was so peaceful on this hill and one could see so far and think far thoughts. Caddie braided the stems of her flowers together into a garland and hung it across the little white fence for Mary. Then she leaned back on last year's autumn leaves and this year's flowers, and fell into a sort of happy daydream.

Presently she heard someone coming up the hill and she sat up to see who it was. Hetty's energetic, small legs were bringing her up the hill, her red pigtails bobbing and shining.

"Oh, bother!" said Caddie, "she's got something to tell."

But today Hetty had nothing to tell. She came up quietly and sat down beside Caddie, her round face flushed with the climb. "I saw you up here, and I thought I'd come too," she said.

"It's nice up here," said Caddie.

"Yes, it is nice," said Hetty. After a while she added: "It's kind of nice to be just us two alone, too, isn't it? Without the boys. But I guess it's more fun for you with the boys."

"Oh, I don't know," said Caddie. "Sometimes I get kind of tired of being with the boys all the time. I came off by myself today."

"Maybe you'd ruther I hadn't come," said Hetty. There was something unexpectedly wistful in her bright eyes.

"Why, no," said Caddie. "I think it's nicer since you came, Hetty. I really do."

A pleased smile brightened Hetty's face. They sat on in silence for a while. But Caddie's mood of vacant daydreaming had passed. Something in Hetty's face had started a whole train of unaccustomed thoughts. She stole occasional glances at the serious, round face, turned now across the farm toward the road which wound away in the distance. It was almost as if Caddie had never seen that little face before. Suddenly she understood for the first time that Hetty was all by herself. Minnie was too young, and Tom, Caddie, and Warren had no room in their adventures for a tagging and tattling little sister. Was her eagerness to be the first to tell only her way of trying to make herself important in the eyes of all the selfish older people? If little Mary had lived—

"Caddie! Look!" cried Hetty, suddenly jumping to her feet and pointing. "It's the circuit rider! He's coming along the road." Caddie's thoughts scattered like frightened birds. She, too, sprang to her feet and focused her eyes on the distant road.

"Sure enough!" she cried. "It's Mr. Tanner! How long he was gone this time! Let's run down and meet him. I want to tell him that I was the one who mended his clock. Come on!"

Away they ran, down the hill, across the newly plowed field, through the barnyard, and into the barn to tell Father.

"Father, the circuit rider's coming!"

"Father, Mr. Tanner's on the road! He'll be here in a minute."

"Bless my soul, I'll be glad to see him," said Father. "It's been a long time, and he's been so far back in the woods. I wonder if he's heard of Lee's surrender?"

Mr. Tanner rode slowly up the lane to the barn. His horse looked tired and muddy. But there was something so strange and sad about Mr. Tanner himself that the children stopped halfway in running to meet him. It was as if he carried bad news for them.

"Hey, Mr. Tanner!" cried Father. "Welcome home again! But you look as if you had not heard the good news. Is it possible that no one has told you the war is ended?"

Mr. Tanner got down slowly, and stood a moment with his hand on his horse's neck, his head bowed. When he spoke, his voice was deep and husky.

"God help us, Mr. Woodlawn!" he said at last. "I have later news than yours. Abraham Lincoln has been shot."

19 · Two Unexpected Heroes

Spring slipped away and it was summer again. The children helped Father and Robert cut and store the wild hay. Then the three adventurers took their buckets and went out into the woods to harvest the summer berries for their mother. There were blueberries for pies and puddings and pin cherries for quivering red jelly. There were Juneberries and wild strawberries, and later there were raspberries and blackberries and thorn apples.

"I guess the Woodlawn family wouldn't have much to eat if it wasn't for us," boasted Warren.

"Oh, yes," said Caddie with a twinkle in her eye, "Mother'd give us turkey."

One day they crossed the river and went as far as Chimney Bluffs, a high, rocky place overlooking the river.

"It's better to go to Chimney Bluffs in the spring or the fall," said Tom. "There's rattlers here in the summer, and we'd better look sharp and keep our ears open or we'll get bit."

The blueberries were thick on Chimney Bluffs and in the excitement of picking them it was hard to remember that one must be on the lookout for rattlesnakes. But, although the children were brave, they were not foolhardy, and life in a wild country had taught them to be cautious. Tom went ahead with a forked stick and the other two followed him, Indian file. They had almost filled their buckets, when Tom found something that filled his heart with joy.

"Goll*ee*-Christmas!" he shouted. "This is as good as the scalp belt!"

The others crowded around him and saw, bleaching in the short grass, the skeleton of a huge snake.

"What a whopper!" yelled Warren.

"I'll bet it's four feet long!" said Tom breathlessly. "Here, you take my berries." With reckless haste he heaped his berries into their buckets and began gathering the vertebrae of the hapless snake into his pail. "Oh, say, I'll string him together and we'll have

another show. Oh, goll*ee!* What a beauty! I wonder
what Katie'll think!"

"Look at the size of his rattle!" marveled Warren
as the last pieces went into Tom's bucket.

He shook it to hear the little dry, buzzing rattle.
Then he dropped it in the bucket, but the little, dry,
buzzing rattle continued.

"Tom! Look!" said Caddie, in a strange, urgent
voice. The boys' eyes followed her pointing finger.
Only a few feet away was coiled a brown and yellow
snake. Its wicked little eyes glinted at them, and its
tail rattled a warning. With berries flying out of
buckets, they fled down the hill. Over rocks and
bushes, helter-skelter, shouting, they ran. If there
were other snakes on Chimney Bluffs that day, they,
too, must have fled away in terror. Tom, Caddie, and
Warren did not stop running until they reached the
river. There they paused a moment to draw breath,
and then they plunged in, clothes and all, with only
their buckets balanced on their heads.

"Well," said Tom, when they were safely at home.
"That's the last time we go to Chimney Bluffs in the
summer. But, oh! crickety! didn't I get a bully
skeleton!"

"You shouldn't have wandered so far away from
home, children," said Mrs. Woodlawn. "Perhaps it's

for lack of work to do here on the farm. I'll see what I can do to remedy that."

The three adventurers exchanged unhappy glances. Berrying was much more to their taste than churning. But churning it was! During the summer when cream was plentiful, Mrs. Woodlawn churned great quantities of butter, packed it and sealed it in brown stone jars, and set the jars away in rows in the cool box which Father had dug and built around the spring at the north of the house. There, with the cold spring water trickling around it, the butter kept fresh until cold weather came, and so they were sure of having butter all the year around. There had been one dreadful summer, which Caddie always remembered as she helped to fill the brown stone jars. Caddie knew that Mother remembered it, too, although she never spoke of it. The butter had been all put up for the summer, and the family had gone to town in the wagon to meet the Little Steamer. That year one of their neighbors had been letting his hogs run loose in the woods. When they returned, they found that these hogs had broken through the fence, knocked the platform off the top of the spring box, upset and broken the butter jars and rolled them in the mud, spoiling what butter they had not eaten. The Woodlawns had stood silent and aghast, looking at the ruin of their winter's butter.

Often their bread was without butter that year, but that was not why the children remembered the calamity so vividly. They remembered it because on that day Mother had cried—the only time that they had ever seen her cry. After that Father had built stronger fences, and the neighbor had been persuaded to shut his hogs in a pen.

Now, when summer woods and fields were at their pleasantest, Miss Parker came back from Durand and opened and swept the schoolhouse. Oh, how tedious it was to go to school in summer! Even *churning* on a cool back porch, with a deep glass of buttermilk to drink afterward, was heavenly compared to school.

Through the open windows of the schoolhouse came the sound of birds and droning bees, and the heavy odors of clover and milkweed in blossom. The eyes of the children kept wandering from their books to the window squares of green and gold where grasshoppers sang and heat shimmered in little wavy lines. Silas Bunn used to slip to the window when Teacher wasn't looking and hang out so far that only his heels and the seat of his trousers were visible to those inside the room. He had done it so often, with no remarks from Teacher, that he no longer took the trouble to be stealthy about it. One day, when he was hanging out, absorbed in watching a spider snare a fly, Miss Parker came up behind him. She stood and looked at him a moment while the children held their breaths, wondering what she would do. Presently she took a firm hold on the seat of Silas's pants and lifted him on out the window. Miss Parker was not very big, but then neither was Silas. She set a surprised and frightened Silas neatly on the ground beneath the window.

"There, Silas," said Miss Parker, "you get up and look all around, and when you have seen all there is to see, come back to school." It did not take Silas long to see all that there was to see. After that he was a wistful looker with the other children, but not a hanger-out. The children's voices droned sleepily through the heat, like the voices of the bees and katydids.

After Tom had sorted and wired together the many little bones of his rattlesnake skeleton, Teacher let him bring it to school and hang it over the map of North America. That made a little break in the monotony, and then there was another break—a more exciting one. A letter came from Boston for Mother from Cousin Annabelle Grey.

I shall be charmed to visit you, dear Aunty Harriet [the letter said]. *Mamma and papa think that my education will not be complete without a view of the majestic open spaces of my native land. Although I*

have recently been finished at the Misses Blodgett's
Seminary for Young Ladies, I, myself, feel that I may
yet be able to acquire some useful information in the
vicissitudes of travel.

"Wow!" said Tom, when Mother read the letter.
"Does she always talk like that?"

"I imagine not," said Mrs. Woodlawn. "But it's a
very pretty letter, isn't it? And what a delicate
penmanship!"

Often over her slate or her reader Caddie's thoughts
wandered to Cousin Annabelle. The pleasure of her
anticipation was sometimes marred by a pang of fear.
What would a girl be like who could write such a
letter? It sounded like a story from *The Mother's Assistant* or *The Young Ladies' Friend*—those tiresome
stories which were so much less interesting than Hans
Andersen's or Tom's. Caddie tried to imagine herself
writing that letter to an aunt in Boston. No, Caddie
Woodlawn would never write a letter like that.
Couldn't she or wouldn't she? She honestly did not
know, but it made her a little ashamed and apprehen-
sive to think about it.

The summer grew hotter and drier. The Indians did
not come back, and Father said it was because they
could read the weather signs and knew that hunting

and fishing would be better in the north. On hot evenings Tom and Caddie used to go down to the lake and
take the canoe out to set lines for fish. Using empty,
corked jugs as floats, they anchored them in several
places on the lake with baited lines attached to them.
In the morning early, before school, they would go
down and pull in the lines, and usually there would be
a nice pike or two for Mrs. Conroy to bake or make
into chowder. John's dog went with them to the lake,
his tongue hanging out and his eyes alert for any
small fish which they might throw him. Just now
John's dog was in disfavor at the farmhouse. He had
bitten the head off one of Clara's pet kittens, and Caddie was the only one who continued to love and defend
him. Like Mary's lamb, he used to follow her to school,
and sit mournfully outside the little building, waiting
until she came out at recess and at noon.

"What a horrid, ugly, ol' Indian dog!" said all the
girls.

But Caddie replied: "He's *mine!*" and she said it so
fiercely that that seemed reason enough why everyone
should like him.

One afternoon John's dog set up a mournful howl
outside the schoolhouse. It was a stifling hot afternoon
and everything was as dry as a tinder box. The sun
had been overcast since early afternoon and the hope

of rain was in everybody's mind. But there was no hint
of rain's freshness in the hot west wind—only a queer,
hot smell. In the middle of the afternoon John's dog
came and scratched at the schoolhouse door and gave
three or four short, troubled barks. When no one paid
him any attention, he came around to the window. By
standing on his hind legs and putting his front paws
on the side of the schoolhouse, he could just manage to
look in the window. He looked around, trying to see
Caddie among the other children, then he put up his
mouth and uttered a long, unhappy howl, followed by
several short barks!

The children began to titter and Miss Parker
rapped sharply on her desk. "Caroline Woodlawn," she
said, "will you please look to your dog?"

Caddie rose obediently and went to the window to
send her dog away. But what she had intended saying
to the dog never came out. Instead she turned back to
the schoolroom, her hands flung in the air, her eyes
wide.

"Teacher! It's a fire! It's a prairie fire. It's coming
here!"

"Fire?" cried the children. They sprang out of
their seats, throwing the quiet schoolroom into a
hubbub.

Miss Parker rapped again on her desk. Her face was

suddenly pale, but she cried out in a strong voice: "Get back into your seats, every one of you! Don't you dare to move until I tell you that you may!" No danger was greater than Teacher's voice, when she spoke like that. Every child but one sank back into his seat. That one was Obediah, who had gone out of the door like a shot at the first word of fire.

Miss Parker took a hasty look out of the window. "Now," she said, "gather your things together and get ready to pass out in the usual way. No running or pushing—just as usual. One—two—three—march!" When they were outside, they broke ranks and scattered before the little licking red tongues of flame that were running through the dry grass toward the schoolhouse.

"Run to Dunnville for help," cried Teacher. "We must save the schoolhouse if we can." Caddie caught the command and raced for Dunnville, with John's dog racing beside her. Miss Parker took up the bucket of water that stood by the schoolroom door. However, one bucket of water does not go very far in a prairie fire, and the spring was some distance down the road.

But a fire fighter was already at work. Obediah, his head down, the smoke swirling all about him, had caught up a flat board and was beating out the fire as fast as he could. When his brother Ashur saw what he

was doing, he caught up a board, too, and ran to join him. The other boys, forgetting their panic in a common purpose, began to imitate the two Jones boys.

"Hey, you," shouted Obediah to Tom, "get a shovel or sumpin' to dig with." In the schoolhouse Tom found the shovel they used to make a path through the snow in winter. He knew what Obediah wanted, and he began to dig and scrape the dry grass away in a trench between the oncoming fire and the schoolhouse. The ground was baked almost as hard as rock and the shovel was not sharp. It was slow work and the sweat stood out all over Tom's round face after a few moments of digging.

"Here!" said Obediah, and he grasped the shovel and thrust his board into Tom's hands. The board was already charred and smoking, but Tom seized it and fell to beating back the fire, while Obediah threw his strength into clearing a trench around the schoolhouse before the fire reached it. Obediah's great, hulking frame, which fitted so badly into the school benches and desks, seemed splendid at last. No grown man could have done braver or harder work than Obediah did that day to save his schoolhouse.

When Caddie came panting back with several men from the store and tavern at Dunnville following her, Obediah and the boys had already succeeded in turning the fire aside. The schoolhouse stood safe and sound on a little island, surrounded by a trench and a ring of blackened and beaten grass. With the help of the men from Dunnville the rest of the fire was extinguished before it reached the town. Then the children came back to school. But there were no more lessons that day.

"Children," said Miss Parker, "you have all been very brave, but one among you has been a hero today, and I want you to salute him. Obediah Jones, please come up here in front."

Grinning a little sheepishly, Obediah came forward. His face was blackened with smoke and his hands were cut and burned, but he had lost his old hang-dog slouch. Obediah stood straight as a man. The little schoolhouse rang with the children's cheers.

"You owe your lives to someone else, too, children," said Miss Parker. She went to the door and opened it.

Indian John's dog slunk in and came and put his head on Caddie's lap. He knew that he did not belong inside, and yet here he was, and, strangely enough, everyone was petting him.

"I hope that you are all properly thankful," said Miss Parker, "and now you may go home. We've had enough for one day."

20 · Alas!
Poor Annabelle!

There were rains after that and things grew green again. And presently it was time for Cousin Annabelle to arrive on the Little Steamer. Mrs. Hyman and Katie had come out to help make the girls' new summer dresses, and Clara and Mother had been in their element, turning the pages of the *Godey's Lady's Book* and talking of muslin, bodices, buttons, and braids.

"Of course," said Clara sadly, "anything we can make here will be sure to be six months behind the fashions in Boston, to say the least; and I do wish I might have hoops for every day."

"I don't!" cried Caddie. "Good gracious, every time I sit down in hoops they fly up and hit me in the nose!"

"That's because you don't know how to manage them," said Clara. "There's an art to wearing hoops, and I suppose you're too much of a tomboy ever to learn it."

"I suppose so," said Caddie cheerfully. But to herself she added: "I'm not really so much of a tomboy as they think. Perhaps I *shall* wear hoops some day, but only when I get good and ready."

Then one day Cousin Annabelle came. The Little Steamer seemed full of her little round-topped trunks and boxes, and, after they had all been carried off, down the gangplank tripped Annabelle Grey herself in her tiny buttoned shoes, with her tiny hat tilted over her nose and its velvet streamers floating out behind. Clara and Caddie had been allowed to come with Mother and Father to meet her, and Caddie suddenly felt all clumsy hands and feet when she saw this delicate apparition.

"Dearest Aunty Harriet, what a pleasure this is!" cried Annabelle in a voice as cultivated as her penmanship. "And this is Uncle John? And these the little cousins? How quaint and rustic it is here! But, just a moment, let me count my boxes. There ought to be seven. Yes, that's right. They're all here. Now we can go."

Father piled the seven boxes in the back of the

wagon and Clara and Caddie climbed in on top of them, while Annabelle sat between Mother and Father, her full skirts billowing over their knees. Above the rattle of the wagon wheels her cultivated voice ran on and on. Clara leaned forward to catch what they were saying and sometimes put in a word of her own, but Caddie sat tongue-tied and uncomfortable, conscious only of her own awkwardness and of a sharp lock on one of Annabelle's boxes which hurt her leg whenever they went over a bump.

When they reached the farm Hetty, Minnie, and the boys ran out and stood in a smiling row beside the wagon. Tom held baby Joe in his arms.

"Dear me!" said Cousin Annabelle, "are these children all yours, Aunty Harriet?"

"There are only seven," said Mother, "and every one is precious."

"Of course! Mother told me there were seven. But they do look such a lot when one sees them all together, don't they?"

"I picked you a nosegay," said Hetty, holding out a rather wilted bunch of flowers which she had been clutching tightly in her warm hands for a long time.

"How very thoughtful of you, little girl," said Annabelle. "But do hold it for me, won't you? I should hate to stain my mitts. You've no idea what a dirty journey this has been, and what difficulty I have had in keeping clean."

"You look very sweet and fresh, my dear," said Mother, "but I'm sure that you must be tired. Come in and take a cup of tea."

Caddie stayed outside a moment to put a quick arm about Hetty's shoulders. "That was an awful pretty nosegay you made, anyway, Hetty," she said.

Hetty's downcast face suddenly shone bright again. "Yes, it was, wasn't it, Caddie? Would you like it?"

"Why, yes, I would. I think it would look real nice here on my new dress, don't you?"

"Oh, it would be lovely, Caddie!"

That evening everyone listened to Annabelle telling about Boston. Mother's eyes shone and her cheeks were pinker than usual. It had been a good many years now since she had seen one of her own kin direct from home. Now she could find out whether Grandma Grey's rheumatism was really better or whether they only wrote that to reassure her. She could find out what pattern of silk Cousin Kitty had chosen for her wedding gown, who had been lecturing in Boston this winter, what new books had come out since the end of the war, why Aunt Phœbe had forgotten to write to her, and a hundred other things that she longed to know, but could never get them to put into letters.

From time to time Father glanced at her happy face, over the old newspapers which Annabelle had brought him. It was only at moments such as this that Father understood how much Mother had given up when she left Boston to come with him to Wisconsin.

But after an hour or so of Boston gossip, Tom grew restless. Both he and Caddie were well tired of Annabelle's city airs.

"Well, I guess Boston's a pretty good place all right, but how about Dunnville?" Tom said.

Cousin Annabelle's silvery laughter filled the room. "Why, Tom, Boston is one of the world's great cities— the only one I'd care to live in, I am sure; and Dunnville—well, it's just too quaint and rustic, but it isn't even on the maps yet."

"Why, Tom," echoed Hetty seriously, "you hadn't ought to have said that. I guess Boston is just like— like Heaven, Tom." Everyone burst out laughing at this, and Cousin Annabelle rose and shook out her flounces, preparatory to going to bed.

"But really, Tom," she said, "I want you to show me *everything* in your savage country. I want to be just as *uncivilized* as you are while I am here. I shall learn to ride horseback and milk the cows—and—and salt the sheep, if that is what you do—and—turn somersaults in the haymow—and—what else do you do?"

"Oh, lots of things," said Tom, and suddenly there was an impish twinkle in his eyes.

"And you, Caroline," said Annabelle, turning to Caddie. "I suppose that you do all of those amusing things, too?"

"Yes, I'm afraid I do, Cousin Annabelle," replied Caddie. She tried to avoid Tom's eyes, but somehow it seemed impossible, and for just an instant an impish twinkle in her own met and danced with the impish twinkle in Tom's.

"You must begin to teach me tomorrow," said Annabelle sweetly. "I'm sure that it will be most interesting, and now, if you will excuse me, I am really quite fatigued."

"Yes, of course, dear Annabelle, and you're to sleep with me," said Clara, linking her arm through Annabelle's and leading her upstairs.

The next morning Tom, Caddie, and Warren had a brief consultation behind the straw stack. They ran through the list of practical jokes which they were used to playing when Uncle Edmund was among them.

"We can make up better ones than most of those," said Tom confidently. "It'll do her good."

"Let's see," said Caddie dreamily. "She wants to ride horseback and salt the sheep and turn somersaults in the haymow. Yes, I think that we can manage."

"Golly! What fun!" chirped Warren, turning a handspring.

When they entered the house, Annabelle had just come bouncing down the stairs, resolved upon being uncivilized for the day. She wore a beautiful new dress which was of such a novel style and cut that Mother and Clara could not admire it enough. Up and down both front and back of the fitted bodice was a row of tiny black jet buttons that stood out and sparkled at you when you looked at them.

"Golly!" said Warren, "you don't need all those buttons to fasten up your dress, do you?"

"Of course not," laughed Annabelle. "They are for decoration. All the girls in Boston are wearing them now, but none of them have as many buttons as I have. I have eight and eighty, and that's six more than Bessie Beaseley and fourteen more than Mary Adams."

"You don't say!" said Tom, and once again he and Caddie exchanged a twinkling glance.

"When shall I have my riding lesson?" asked Annabelle after breakfast.

"Right away, if you like," said Caddie pleasantly.

Clara stayed to help Mother, and Minnie was playing with baby Joe, but Hetty came with the others.

"Hadn't you better stay with Mother, Hetty?" said Tom in his kindest voice.

But, no, Hetty wanted to see the riding lesson.

Annabelle chattered vivaciously of how much better everything was done in Boston, while Tom went into the barn to bring out the horse.

"Why, Tom," cried Hetty, when he returned, "that's not Betsy, that's Pete."

Pete was perfectly gentle in appearance, but he had one trick which had kept the children off his back for several years.

"Hetty," said Caddie firmly, "we must have perfect quiet while anyone is learning to ride. If you can't be perfectly quiet, we'll have to send you right back to the house."

"I suppose he bucks," said Cousin Annabelle. "All Western horses do, don't they? Shall I be hurt?"

"He's pretty gentle," said Tom. "You better get on and you'll find out."

"Bareback and astride?" quavered Annabelle. "Dear me! How quaint and rustic!"

Caddie and Tom helped her on.

"He hasn't started bucking yet," said Annabelle proudly. "I *knew* that I should be a good rider!"

"Just touch him with the switch a little," advised Tom.

At the touch of the switch, Pete swung into a gentle canter, but instead of following the road, he made for a particular shed at the back of the barn. It was Pete's one accomplishment.

"How do I pull the rein to make him go the other way?" queried Annabelle, but already Pete was gathering momentum and, before they could answer, he had swung in under the low shed, scraped Annabelle neatly off into the dust, and was standing peacefully at rest inside the shed picking up wisps of hay.

Annabelle sat up in a daze. The little straw sun hat which she had insisted on wearing was over one ear and she looked very comical indeed.

"I don't yet understand what happened," she said politely. "I thought that I was going along so well. In Boston, I'm sure the horses never behave like that."

"Would you like to try another horse?" said Tom.

"Oh no!" said Annabelle hastily. "Not today, at least. Couldn't we go and salt the sheep now, perhaps?"

"Do you think we could, Tom?" asked Caddie doubtfully.

"Why, yes, I believe we could," said Tom kindly. "Here let me help you up, Cousin Annabelle."

"I'll get the salt," shouted Warren, racing into the barn.

Hetty looked on in silence, her eyes round with surprise. Annabelle rose, a bit stiffly, and brushed the back of her beautiful dress.

"She's not a crybaby at any rate," thought Caddie to herself. "Maybe it's kind of mean to play another trick on her."

But Warren had already returned with the salt, and he and Tom, with Annabelle between them, were setting out for the woodland pasture where Father kept the sheep. Caddie hastened to catch up with them, and Hetty, still wondering, tagged along behind.

"Will they eat out of my hand, if I hold it for them?" asked Annabelle, taking the chunk of salt from Warren.

"Sure," said Tom, "they're crazy about salt."

"But you mustn't *hold* it," said Hetty, coming up panting. "You must lay it down where the sheep can get it."

"Now, Hetty," said Caddie, "what did I tell you about keeping perfectly quiet?"

"You do just as you like, Annabelle," said Tom kindly.

"Well, of course," said Annabelle, "I should prefer to hold it and let the cunning little lambs eat it right out of my hands."

"All right," said Tom, "you go in alone then, and

we'll stay outside the fence here where we can watch you."

"It's so nice of you to let me do it," said Cousin Annabelle. "How do you call them?"

Tom uttered a low persuasive call—the call to salt. He uttered it two or three times, and sheep began coming from all parts of the woods into the open pasture.

Annabelle stood there expectantly, holding out the salt, a bright smile on her face. "We don't have sheep in Boston," she said. But almost immediately the smile began to fade.

The sheep were crowding all around her, so close that she could hardly move; they were treading on her toes and climbing on each other's backs to get near her. Frightened, she held the salt up out of their reach, and then they began to try to climb up *her* as if she had been a ladder. There was a perfect pandemonium of bleating and baaing, and above this noise rose Annabelle's despairing shriek.

"Drop the salt and run," called Tom, himself a little frightened at the success of his joke. But running was not an easy matter with thirty or forty sheep around her, all still believing that she held the salt. At last poor Annabelle succeeded in breaking away and they helped her over the fence. But, when she was safe on the other side, everybody stopped and looked at her in amazement. The eight and eighty sparkling jet buttons had disappeared from her beautiful frock. The sheep had eaten them!

"Oh! my buttons!" cried Annabelle. "There were eight and eighty of them—six more than Bessie Beaseley had! And where is my sun hat?"

Across the fence in the milling crowd of sheep, the wicked Woodlawns beheld with glee Annabelle's beautiful sun hat rakishly dangling from the left horn of a fat old ram.

21 · *Father Speaks*

If Annabelle had rushed home crying and told Mother,
the Woodlawn children would not have been greatly
surprised. But there seemed to be more in Annabelle
than met the eye.

"What a quaint experience!" she said. "They'll
hardly believe it when I tell them about it in Boston."
Her voice was a trifle shaky, but just as polite as ever,
and she went right upstairs, without speaking to Clara
or Mother, and changed to another dress. That evening
she was more quiet than she had been the night before
and she had almost nothing to say about the superi-
ority of her native city over the rest of the uncivilized
world. Caddie noticed with remorse that Annabelle

walked a little stiffly, and she surmised that the ground had not been very soft at the place where Pete had scraped her off.

"I wish I hadn't promised Tom to play that next trick on her," Caddie thought to herself. "Maybe he'll let me off."

But Tom said, no, it was a good trick and Annabelle had asked for it, and Caddie had promised to do her part, and she had better go through with it.

"All right," said Caddie.

After all it was a good trick and Annabelle *had* asked for it.

"Let's see," said Tom the next day. "You wanted to turn somersaults in the haymow, didn't you, Cousin Annabelle?"

"Well, I suppose that's one of the things one always does on a farm, isn't it?" said Cousin Annabelle, a trifle less eagerly than she had welcomed their suggestions of the day before. The beautiful eight-and-eighty-button dress had not appeared today. Annabelle had on a loose blouse over a neat, full skirt. "Of course, I never turn somersaults in Boston, you understand. It's so very quaint and rustic."

"Of course, we understand that," said Caddie.

"But out here where you have lots of hay—"

"It's bully fun!" yelled Warren.

"Now, Hetty," directed Tom, "you better stay at

home with Minnie. A little girl like you might fall down the ladder to the mow and hurt herself."

"Me fall down the haymow ladder?" demanded Hetty in amazement. "Why, Tom Woodlawn, you're just plumb crazy!"

"Well, run into the house then and fetch us some cookies," said Tom, anxious to be rid of Hetty's astonished eyes and tattling tongue. Hetty departed reluctantly with a deep conviction that she was missing out on something stupendous.

When she returned a few moments later with her hands full of cookies, she could hear them all laughing and turning somersaults in the loft above. She made haste to climb the ladder and peer into the loft. It was darkish there with dust motes dancing in the rays of light that entered through the chinking. But Hetty could see quite plainly, and what she saw was Caddie slipping an egg down the back of Annabelle's blouse, just as Annabelle was starting to turn a somersault.

"I can turn them every bit as well as you can already," said Annabelle triumphantly, and then she turned over, and then she sat up with a surprised and stricken look upon her face, and then she began to cry!

"Oh, it's squishy!" she sobbed. "You're horrid and mean. I didn't mind falling off the horse or salting the sheep, but oh, this—this—*this* is *squishy!*"

Hetty climbed down from the haymow and ran to the house as fast as she could go.

"Mother, if you want to see something, you just come here with me as fast as you can," she cried.

On the way to the barn she gave Mrs. Woodlawn a brief but graphic account of the riding lesson and the sheep salting. When they reached the haymow, Annabelle was still sobbing.

"Oh, Aunty Harriet!" she cried. "I don't know what it is, but it's squishy. I can't—oh dear! I *can't* bear squishy things!"

"You poor child!" said Mrs. Woodlawn, examining the back of Annabelle's blouse, and then, in an ominous voice, she announced: "It's egg." With a good deal of tenderness Mother got Annabelle to the house and put her into Clara's capable hands. Then she turned with fury on the three culprits. But it was Caddie whom she singled out for punishment.

"Caroline Woodlawn, stand forth!" she cried. Caddie obeyed.

"It was only a joke, Mother," she said in a quivering voice. Mrs. Woodlawn took a little riding whip which hung behind the kitchen door and struck Caddie three times across the legs.

"Now go to your bed and stay until morning. You shall have no supper."

"Ma, it was as much my fault as hers," cried Tom, his ruddy face gone white.

"No, Tom," said Mrs. Woodlawn. "I cannot blame *you* so much. But that a *daughter* of mine should so far forget herself in her hospitality to a guest—that she should be such a hoyden as to neglect her proper duties as a lady! Shame to her! Shame! No punishment that I can invent would be sufficient for her."

As Caddie went upstairs, she saw Father standing in the kitchen door and she knew that he had witnessed her disgrace. But she knew, too, that he would do nothing to soften the sentence which Mother had spoken, for it was an unwritten family law that one parent never interfered with the justice dealt out by the other.

For hours Caddie tossed about on her bed. The upper room was hot and close, but an even hotter inner fire burned in Caddie. She had some of her mother's quick temper, and she was stung by injustice. She would have accepted punishment without question if it had been dealt out equally to the boys. But the boys had gone free! All the remorse and the resolves to do better, which had welled up in her as soon as she had seen Annabelle's tears, were dried up now at the injustice of her punishment. Hot and dry-eyed, she tossed about on the little bed where she had spent so

many quiet hours. At last she got up and tied a few
things which she most valued into a towel. She put
them under the foot of her mattress and lay down
again. Later she would slip down to the kitchen and
get a loaf of bread and Father's old water bottle which
she would fill at the spring. At least they could not
begrudge her that much. They would soon cease to
miss her. Perhaps they would adopt Annabelle in her
place.

Her anger cooled a little in the fever of making
plans. It would have been much easier if she had
known just where the Indians were. But at this season
the woods were full of berries and there would soon be
nuts. John's dog would protect her and she could live
a long time in the woods until she could join the Indians. She knew that they would take her in, and then
she would never have to grow into that hateful thing
which Mother was always talking about—a lady. A
lady with fine airs and mincing walk who was afraid
to go out into the sun without a hat òr a sunshade! A
lady, who made samplers and wore stays and was
falsely polite no matter how she felt!

A soft blue twilight fell, and still Caddie tossed, hot,
resentful, and determined. There was the clatter of supper dishes down below, and no one relented enough to
send her a bite of bread. A velvet darkness followed

the twilight and, through the window, summer stars began to twinkle. Presently Hetty and Minnie came up to bed. Hetty came and stood by Caddie's bed and looked at her. Caddie could feel the long, wistful look, but she did not stir or open her eyes. Hetty was a tattletale. It was torture to have to lie so still, but at last the little sisters were breathing the regular breath of sleep, and Caddie could toss and turn again as much as she pleased. She must keep awake now until the house was all still and the lights out, and then she would be free to run away. Her heart beat fast, and with every beat something hot and painful seemed to throb in her head. A cooler breeze began to come in at the window. How long it took the house to grow quiet tonight! How tiresome they were! They wouldn't even go to bed and let her run away!

Then the door creaked a little on its hinges, there was a glimmer of candlelight, and Father came in. He went first and looked at Minnie and Hetty. He put a lock of hair back from Minnie's forehead and pulled the sheet up over Hetty's shoulder. Then he came and stood by Caddie's bed. She lay very still with tightly closed eyes so that Father should think her asleep. It had fooled Hetty, but Father knew more than most people did. He put the candle down and sat on the side of the bed and took one of Caddie's hot hands in his cool ones. The he began to speak in his nice quiet voice, without asking her to wake up or open her eyes or look at him.

"Perhaps Mother was a little hasty today, Caddie," he said. "She really loves you very much, and, you see, she expects more of you than she would of someone she didn't care about. It's a strange thing, but somehow we expect more of girls than of boys. It is the sisters and wives and mothers, you know, Caddie, who keep the world sweet and beautiful. What a rough world it would be if there were only men and boys in it, doing things in their rough way! A woman's task is to teach them gentleness and courtesy and love and kindness. It's a big task, too, Caddie—harder than cutting trees or building mills or damming rivers. It takes nerve and courage and patience, but good women have those things. They have them just as much as the men who build bridges and carve roads through the wilderness. A woman's work is something fine and noble to grow up to, and it is just as important as a man's. But no man could ever do it so well. I don't want you to be the silly, affected person with fine clothes and manners whom folks sometimes call a lady. No, that is not what I want for you, my little girl. I want you to be a woman with a wise and understanding heart, healthy in body and honest in mind.

Do you think you would like to be growing up into that woman now? How about it, Caddie, have we run with the colts long enough?"

There was a little silence, and the hot tears which had not wanted to come all day were suddenly running down Caddie's cheeks unheeded into the pillow.

"You know, Caddie," added Father gently and half-apologetically, "you know I'm sort of responsible for you, honey. I was the one who urged Mother to let you run wild, because I thought it was the finest way to make a splendid woman of you. And I still believe that, Caddie."

Suddenly Caddie flung herself into Mr. Woodlawn's arms.

"Father! Father!"

It was all she could say, and really there was nothing more that needed saying. Mr. Woodlawn held her a long time, his rough beard pressed against her cheek. Then with his big hands, which were so delicate with clockwork, he helped her to undress and straighten the tumbled bed. Then he kissed her again and took his candle and went away. And now the room was cool and pleasant again, and even Caddie's tears were not unpleasant, but part of the cool relief she felt. In a few moments she was fast asleep.

But something strange had happened to Caddie in the night. When she awoke she knew that she need not be afraid of growing up. It was not just sewing and weaving and wearing stays. It was something more thrilling than that. It was a responsibility, but, as Father spoke of it, it was a beautiful and precious one, and Caddie was ready to go and meet it. She looked at the yellow sunshine on the floor and she knew that she had slept much longer than she usually did. Both Hetty's and Minnie's bed were empty, but as soon as Caddie began to stir around, Hetty came in as if she had been waiting outside the door.

"Oh, say, Caddie," she said, "I'm awful sorry I went

and told on you yesterday. Honest, I am. I never thought you'd get it so hard, and I'll tell you what, I'm not going to be a tattler ever any more, I'm not. But, say, Caddie, I wanted to be the first to tell you Father took Tom and Warren out to the barn yesterday afternoon and he gave 'em both a thrashing. He said it wasn't fair that you should have all the punishment when the same law had always governed you all, and Tom said so, too, although he yelled good and plenty when he was being thrashed."

"It's all right, Hetty," said Caddie. "I guess we won't be playing any more silly jokes on people."

"What's this?" asked Hetty, pulling at the corner of a queer bundle that stuck out under the corner of Caddie's mattress. Out came a knotted towel with an odd assortment of Caddie's treasures rattling around inside.

"Oh, that!" said Caddie, untying the knots and putting the things away. "Those are just some things I was looking at yesterday when I had to stay up here alone."

22 · A Letter
with a Foreign Stamp

That day everything went on as usual. Caddie was
grateful to them for that. Mother gave her a brief
smile and then went on about her morning duties as if
nothing had happened. Father had put the boys to
work at some useful task in the barn. Under the pine
trees Clara and Annabelle had set up the quilting
frame and were busily at work on the quilt which
Clara had been piecing all winter.

Caddie stood in the doorway and looked out at them.
She was not sure how the girl who couldn't bear
"squishy" things would treat her today.

"Oh, Caddie, come and see," cried Clara. "Cousin
Annabelle has taught me the loveliest new quilting
pattern. It's a rose and scroll."

Caddie came and looked. She stood with her feet wide apart and her hands in her apron pockets like a boy. But for once she was not scornful of women's skill. "Do you think I could learn how?" she asked.

"Of course you could," said Annabelle with a generous smile. "Look here, I'll give you my needle and you shall sit beside me and learn."

So Caddie's awkward fingers took up the needle, and, when Father came by a little later, he smiled at her and nodded his head in approval.

"I guess if I can mend clocks, I ought to be able to quilt," said Caddie a little defiantly, and nobody contradicted her, because she was quilting very well. By noon she was quite as good as Clara or Annabelle and so pleased with herself that she thought quilting one of the greatest sports in the world. When Tom and Warren came up from the barn, she hailed them enthusiastically and began to exhibit her skill.

"Golly! I could do that, too!" said Tom. "Girls think they're so smart with their tiny stitches. Where's a needle?"

"Me, too!" said Warren, and before Clara knew what was happening to her precious quilt, the boys had taken possession, and the three erstwhile adventurers were making riotous scrolls and roses all over it.

"Mother," she complained, running breathless into the kitchen, "you've got to make them stop. Their hands are all dirty!"

"Let be! Let be, Clara," said Mrs. Woodlawn, smiling. "The quilt will wash. The quilt will wash."

So it turned out that, when Caddie began to learn to be a housewife, the boys became housewives, too. Of course, they wouldn't have admitted it for worlds, but, after all, the three of them had had their fun together for so long that it was hard to break the habit. The kitchen often rang now with their shouts of laughter, and Mrs. Conroy complained that they were always under foot. But their mother only smiled and nodded.

"Caddie's beginning to take an interest in the house," she said. "That's enough for me. A little housework will not harm the boys."

Thus life went on for about a week, and then something happened which was strange and exciting.

Father had been to the mill at Eau Galle and on the return had gone to Dunnville to get what mail the Little Steamer had brought in that day. When he drove up the lane to the house, the children were all out under the pines in front of the house where they often spent the hot August afternoons. Usually Father had some gay remark to call out to them, and usually they swarmed around him for a ride to the barn. But today,

when they came clamoring for a ride, it seemed as if
Father did not see them. His face had an odd look,
which made him appear somehow a stranger, and in his
hand he held a large envelope on which the seal was
broken.

"Tom," he said, tossing the reins to his son, "put
up the horses." One look at Father's strange face and
Tom obeyed without a word. Father strode across the
grass and opened the front door. "Harriet!" he called,
"Harriet, come into the parlor with me."

The children gasped. The parlor was a sacred room,
used only for weddings and funerals, or Christmas day
or special visitors, or when the circuit rider held a
neighborhood prayer meeting. It was a special-occa-
sion room. But it had one other use, and that was
special, too. When Father and Mother wanted to speak
together very privately and on important matters,
they went into the parlor and closed the door behind
them. They did this now, and the young Woodlawns
stood outside and wondered.

"Did you see the queer, big letter he had?" asked
Hetty. "I guess that's what they're talking about."

"It had foreign stamps on it," said Caddie. "I noticed. They weren't United States'."

"I saw," said Cousin Annabelle, "and I know what
they were. They were English. I know because
Mamma has a cousin who lives in England, and she

sends us letters. Yes, it must have been a letter from England! But whoever would be writing to Uncle John from across seas?"

The Woodlawn children looked at each other with startled faces.

"Our father was born in England, you know," said Caddie slowly, "but I can't guess who would be writing him from there." Tom came back from "putting up" the horses, and they all sat around the doorstep, unable to take up their play again where they had left it. Only Cousin Annabelle seemed unaffected by Father's strangeness. Having thought of England, her cultivated voice rambled on and on in praise of Boston and England. According to Annabelle, England was very nearly as well civilized and delightful as Boston, and, if she were not fortunate enough to marry a Boston clergyman, she thought that an English lord would perhaps do just as well.

"Children!" They turned to see Mother standing behind them in the doorway. Her cheeks were flushed and her eyes bright. "Children, your father wishes to speak to you in the parlor. Annabelle, dear, don't you want to run to the spring and get yourself a cool drink? The children will be out again in a moment."

"Us in the *parlor!*" whispered Warren. "Golly! He must have sumpin' to say!"

Yes, he had. Father sat behind a little table on

which was spread the open letter which had come across the sea. His face was very grave.

"Children," he said, "we have come to a crossroad in our lives. Today I have received a letter from a source which I had thought closed to me. Once this letter could have meant a great deal to me, but now it has come almost too late."

"Oh, no, Johnny!" cried Mother quickly.

"Perhaps Mother is right," he went on. "The letter can still do much for us if we wish it. Children, an uncle, whom I have never seen, has died in England. He was Lord Woodlawn after my grandfather. Since his death, it appears that the family lawyers have spent some time in tracing his successor. At last they have found him. He turns out to be the son of a little seamstress, a boy who used to dance in red breeches and clogs to keep from going hungry. It seems, however oddly, that *I* may be the next Lord Woodlawn."

"*You*, Father!" the children cried, and Clara clasped her hands and said: "Oh, the big house with the peacocks, Father, will it be yours?"

"Yes, the big house with the peacocks, Clara," said Father slowly.

Caddie thought of the big house with the peacocks, too, and she tried to see in her mind just how it looked. But try as she would to see it clearly, the iron bars of a closed gate were always between, just as they had been when Father had first described it.

"There is one condition, however," continued Father, "which I must tell you about. The title and estates in England come to me only if I will give up my American citizenship and all my American connections and return to England to live. This requirement was a part of the late Lord Woodlawn's will, and if I do not wish to comply with it, the land and title will pass on to another more distant relative who is living now in England."

"But, of course, you will," said Mother and Clara together.

"I suppose it would be foolish not to," said Father slowly, and he passed his hand across his forehead as though he were brushing away a cobweb or an unruly bit of hair. Then he folded the letter and put it back in the envelope and stood up, smiling. "In any case our decision must not be hasty," he said. "We must be sure that we are right."

"But it seems to me in a case like this that there can be only one right thing to do!" cried Mother warmly.

Father laid his hand on her arm, and looked deeply into her eyes. "Think, Harriet. Think before you speak," he said.

"Couldn't we ever come back here to the farm?" asked Tom.

"No, Tom."

"Who'd see to the mill at Eau Galle?"

"They'd get another man. The machinery is all installed. Anyone else could keep it in order."

"Would we have to leave Betsy and the animals?" asked Caddie.

"Yes, Caddie. Probably there would be many fine horses awaiting us in England."

Then another thought occurred to Caddie. "Father, how soon would we have to go? Would it be before John came back for his dog and scalp belt?"

"Yes, Caddie, I think it would. If we go, it will be soon."

"*If!*" cried Clara. "Father, how can you say an *if* to such a splendid thing!"

"It is only right to look at all the sides of an important question, Clara."

When they came out into the sunshine again, they were a little dazzled. The parlor had been dark and cool, and, in the few moments they had stood there in dark coolness, the whole future had suddenly changed for the little Woodlawns. How strange, how unbelievable it was! No wonder they blinked at the sun when they came out. But suddenly Tom saw something which brought him out of his daze. Hetty was setting off across the fields toward Maggie Bunn's.

"Bring her back," yelled Tom, and Caddie and Warren raced along with him to catch her.

They weren't long in overtaking her, and Tom said fiercely: "You hold your tongue, Hetty. Don't you go telling anyone we're English until you're good and sure."

"English?" said Hetty. "But we aren't English, Tom!"

"We will be if we go back there. Didn't you know that, you little silly?"

Hetty stopped struggling to be free, and looked earnestly from one face to another. "Will we? I thought we'd always be Americans. Then, I guess, I don't want to tell after all," she said, and the four of them went silently back to the house together.

That evening at supper Annabelle, Clara, and Mother did most of the talking. Annabelle, particularly, was full of most delightful plans for their life in England.

"Of course, you shall be presented to the Queen," she said, "and there will be balls and concerts and all manner of elegant things. Just think of the splendid clothes you can wear! The very latest fashions and more buttons than anyone else in London if you like,

and no sheep to eat them off, and all the handsome
noblemen simply languishing for dances with you. Oh,
I do so envy you, you lucky girls! I do hope you will
have me to visit you in England! Perhaps I shall
change my mind about the Boston clergyman, after
all, and have the English lord for first choice. Wasn't
it funny that I should have said that this very afternoon, and all the time Uncle John already knew he was
to be one? Fancy an English lord coming from Dunnville! Was ever anything more absurd?"

Father said very little, and once, when Caddie
glanced at him, she caught a troubled look in his eyes.
It made the uncomfortable little ache in her own heart
sharper.

After supper Caddie and the boys slipped out to the

barn. Robert Ireton sat on a milking stool, tilted back against the barn, and strummed his banjo. His voice was plaintive tonight. He was singing about a beautiful maiden who had died of a broken heart and been buried under a weeping willow tree. Caddie sat on a loose pile of hay, her arms clasped around her knees. Above her the dark sky glittered and sparkled with thousands of stars. The Milky Way was a broad, white path across the sky. There was the North Star and another star which she loved because it was so bright. She did not know its name, but she had always called it hers. There would be stars in England, but would they be so bright, so beautiful? The smell of clover and new hay tugged at her heart. Would anything in England smell as sweet? And, when Indian John came back to find the treasures he had left with her, would she be gone?

Here under the bright stars, while Robert strummed and sang, Caddie knew that her old, wild past was ended. But suddenly she knew, too, that she wanted the future, whatever it might hold, to be here in the country that she loved, and not among strangers in a strange land.

23 · *Pigeons or Peacocks?*

The members of the family appeared on time for breakfast the next morning, and everyone wore an air of strangeness and expectancy. They knew that today Father would make his decision about going back to England, and until the decision was made they felt ill at ease and somehow like a group of strangers sitting together at the familiar breakfast table. Only Annabelle was perfectly at ease.

"Tom," she said, looking at him with a new interest in her bright eyes, "when you are an English lord, you must not forget your little cousin Annabelle."

"If you mean that you've given up your Boston clergyman," said Tom bluntly, "you needn't count on me, Annabelle. I've got *my* girl all picked."

"Tom! What nonsense!" said Mother. "Go on and eat your porridge."

"I know! I know! I know!" buzzed Hetty. "Tom loves Ka—" Tom reached hastily for the bread and, by some mysterious accident, upset Hetty's glass of milk into her lap, so that the object of Tom's affections was never publicly revealed.

During the confusion of mopping up Hetty, Caddie sat silent. She had dreamed last night about England. There had been peacocks and towers and moats, and it had seemed that the Woodlawn children were to be presented to the Queen, but then all of the others had vanished and only Caddie had gone on alone, and then she had found herself holding the hand of a little boy —such a funny little boy with a sailor suit and a wide hat and red hair, and the little boy had been crying because he was hungry. And, when they had reached the Queen's palace, there had been a great barred gate, and through the gate they could see that the Queen had peacocks, too, but they could not get through the gate, and then soldiers had come and driven them away, and Caddie had wakened up and found that it was morning.

Father's voice broke through the memory of her dream. Caddie turned and looked at him, and she thought that he was nicer sitting thus at the head of his simple table than he could ever be in any other place.

"I have been thinking," he said, "that you children are old enough to have some part in the decision which we must make today. It would hardly be fair for me alone, or for Mother and me, to say, without consulting you, either that you must give up your American citizenship and return to England or that you should remain here, giving up a good deal of money and a high position in England. After all, Mother and I have already lived a half of our lives, and they've been worth the living, haven't they, Harriet?"

Mother smiled tremulously and nodded at him.

"But you young ones have all of your lives before you, and you already have some ideas of what you wish to make of them. It would be a pity for someone else to make a wrong decision for you. So I think it best that we should take a family vote. Since we are still on American soil and have always considered ourselves good Americans, we shall vote in the American way by written ballot. That is, each child shall decide for himself what he wishes to do. Then, without telling anyone else what he has decided, he shall write 'Go' or 'Stay' on a piece of paper which he shall then fold and place between the leaves of the family Bible in the parlor. We shall vote this afternoon at four o'clock, and, in the meantime, I want you to discuss it among yourselves and to ask Mother and me as many questions as you like, and, above all, I want you to think each for yourself: 'What will be best for my future? Where shall I be most useful and happy?'"

"Shall I vote, too, Papa?" asked little Minnie, climbing onto Mr. Woodlawn's knee and looking earnestly into his face.

"Yes, you, too, little Minnie. Every Woodlawn shall vote except baby Joe, and his future we others must decide among us."

At mention of his name the baby bounced in his high chair and banged his spoon upon his tray.

"You and I shall not be allowed to vote, baby Joe," said Annabelle, "but never you mind, you'll be a little English gentleman before the day is over, I'll be bound."

"Goo! goo!" said baby Joe and showed his two new teeth in a pink smile.

Then for a long time Father spoke to them quietly and earnestly, like an impartial judge, setting forth the advantages and the disadvantages of this move. He spoke of England more warmly than they had ever heard him speak before, picturing its beauties and the high place which they would be called to fill there. Then he spoke of America, and he did not say as many

fine things of it as he had often said in the past, and
Caddie knew why. It was because his heart belonged
here in Wisconsin and he did not wish to let his own
preference prejudice his children. But he did speak
briefly of the freedom which belonged to them in a
new country, and he said that, although they might
never be rich or famous in America, they would have
the satisfaction of knowing that what they had they
had made for themselves.

"An inherited fortune is never quite one's own,"
said Father slowly, "and yet I want you to understand
that money and power are also great things, and that
great good may come of them, if they are wisely
handled."

Then he pushed back his chair from the table and
took his hat and went out to see that the horses had a
measure of oats.

"Do you think that Father wants to go back and
be a lord?" asked Tom, as he and Caddie and Warren
walked away to the lake.

"I guess he doesn't want us to know what he
wants," said Caddie in a low voice. "He'd rather we
made up our own minds."

"I can't see Father going back there where they
treated him so badly once," said Tom. "Father's the
kind of man who likes to do things for himself. I don't

s'pose that English lords mend clocks and feed horses and put locks on guns for Indians, do you?"

"They don't have to!" shouted Warren.

"Well, Father doesn't *have* to either, but I think he'd miss it if he didn't do it."

"I think that Father likes to be at the front of things," said Caddie. "He likes to be free and help build new places. I think he'd rather go on west than go back to an old country where everything is finished."

"I would, too," said Tom. "I'd rather build a new mill in America than live in a castle in England that somebody who'd died hundreds of years ago had had the fun of building. That's how I feel."

"Me, too," said Warren.

"I guess we three'll vote the same," said Caddie, "but Mother and Clara and Hetty and Minnie will all be on the other side, and I don't know about Father. What he wants won't matter so much as what he thinks would be best for *us*. And, you know, he likes to make Mother happy."

They climbed onto the raft and Tom pushed off from shore. John's dog rode with them, his head on Caddie's knee.

"Poor fellow!" said Caddie. "I don't know what John'll think if I can't look after you till he gets back."

A cloud of gloom floated along with them as they went down the lake on that bright August morning.

It was almost four o'clock, and the Woodlawn children had washed their hands and faces and smoothed their hair as if they were getting ready for a party.

"Just practicing up to be little lords and ladies," said Annabelle, who was as much excited as the rest of them, and even Tom was too distraught to answer her.

Caddie had gone off by herself to sit under a tree until Father should call her in to vote. She had closed her eyes, because the bees and birds and crickets sounded so much louder when she did, and it was fun to listen to them and try to tell from which direction each sound came. Soon, perhaps, she would be hearing English sounds. Suddenly a hot little hand was thrust into hers and she opened her eyes in surprise to see Hetty gazing earnestly into her face.

"Caddie, I'm going to vote like you do, did you know that?"

"How do you know how I'm going to vote?" asked Caddie. "We're not supposed to tell."

"Oh, I could guess that," said Hetty gravely. "You like it here better than any place, and so do I. I want to be an American."

Suddenly Caddie gave the round cheek a kiss. She had not remembered to kiss Hetty for a long time.

"Hetty," she said, "no matter whether we go to England or stay in Wisconsin, let's be better chums, shall we?"

At four o'clock they went into the parlor and Father gave them all slips of paper exactly alike. There were pen and ink on the table beside the big Bible, and each member of the family wrote something on his or her slip, dried it, folded it, and placed it somewhere in the Bible. Father and Mother had slips of paper like the children, and they did the same. Minnie took longest, because she had only just learned how to print and it had taken Hetty most of the morning to teach her how to print "Go" and "Stay." But everyone waited quietly until she had finished.

"She must be writing 'Stay,'" whispered Hetty into Caddie's ear. "She can't do *s* and *y* very fast. 'Go' wouldn't take her half so long, unless she's forgotten how."

Caddie's heart began to beat more quickly. What if Minnie *did* vote 'Stay"? Hetty had voted to stay. That would make five on their side! Of course Clara and Mother would be on the other side, and no one knew what Father would vote. Caddie knew that Mother's and Father's and even Clara's vote would count for more than theirs, because they were only the "young ones." Nevertheless for the first time today she began to hope. She found herself shivering with excitement.

Father took up the big Bible and looked through it until he had found eight slips of paper. He unfolded the first paper and in a low, clear voice read: "Stay."

One by one three more slips were unfolded and each one said "Stay."

"Those are ours, I guess," whispered Hetty, but Caddie squeezed her hand and said "Hush!" for Father was unfolding the fifth slip of paper.

"Go," read Father in the same steady voice.

Tom and Warren shuffled their feet restlessly. Tom seemed to hear Annabelle's sweet voice saying: "Practicing up to be little lords and ladies," and he kicked out viciously at a rag rug which his restless feet had scuffed into a roll.

Father unfolded the last three papers quickly and looked at them. Then he read them out: "Stay—stay —stay."

"Hooray!" yelled Warren.

But nobody else spoke for a moment. The solemnity of the occasion still held them spellbound.

"There is only one vote to go," said Father slowly.

"That one's mine!" cried Clara. "Give it here and I'll tear it up. I don't want to go to England either!"

"But, Harriet," said Father gravely, taking Mother's hand, "you wanted to go, my dear. Are you doing this for my sake?"

"No, Johnny, I did it all for myself. We're all so

happy here, and we might be wretched there. I never knew how much I loved it here until I had to choose— better than England . . . better than Boston! Home is where you are, Johnny!" Suddenly she burst into tears and flung herself into Mr. Woodlawn's arms.

"Hattie! Hattie! My little Harriet!" cried Father, holding her close and kissing her.

The children stood around with gaping eyes and mouths. Stranger even than an inheritance from England it was, to see Mother crying and Father kissing her.

24 · Travelers Return

It seemed to Caddie Woodlawn that she had never known a more beautiful autumn than the one which followed. Goldenrod and asters bloomed yellow and purple and lavender along the side of every road, and swept in bright waves across the fields to the woods. In the woods the oaks put on their gayest colors. Every shade of red they flung against the clear blue sky, from a soft pinkish lavender to deepest crimson, and the silver birches trembled and shivered in their thinning gold.

Perhaps it was not really a more beautiful autumn than many others had been. Perhaps the difference was in Caddie herself. Certainly she saw things now with wide-open eyes, and Wisconsin had never seemed so sweet to her as now, since she had been in danger of losing it.

One day the Indians came back, and John rode in at the gate and left his pony in the barnyard. Mother had just baked apple pie again, and John came in and sat at the kitchen table and ate. He had no words to tell them of the strange, far wilderness where he had been, what game he had caught, what leafy trails mottled with sunshine he had traveled, what portages and shining lakes he had seen. All he said was "John him back," and ate his pie in silence. But something of the beauty and mystery of far-off places hung about him, and Caddie was glad that she was there to greet him.

His dog sniffed curiously about his legs and moved uneasily back and forth between his master and Caddie. To whom did he belong? To the little girl who had nursed his lame foot and fed and petted him? Or to the tall, brown man who smelled of buckskin and birch smoke and all the strange, wild things that crept and scampered in the woods?

When John had eaten, he took from his bag a pair of moccasins, decorated with the brightly dyed quills of porcupine, and held them out to Caddie. They were just her size and very beautiful.

"Oh, John!" she cried. "Thank you! Thank you!" But John had nothing more to say. He spoke in deeds. He took his scalp belt, grunted to his dog, and mounted his pony.

But now John's dog was confronted with a problem. He ran a little way with his master, then he came back and gazed, whining, into Caddie's face. Caddie was irresolute, too. If she put her arms around him and patted him, she knew that he would stay. She summoned up her courage.

"Go!" she cried, pointing to John. "Go with your master!" The dog gave her a long, questioning look, and then he turned and trotted away behind the Indian pony.

"And so that's that," said Caddie softly to herself, and she was a little sad and a little glad.

But there were other travelers making their way through the wilderness to the Woodlawn farm. The circuit rider had turned his horse that way again, and he was thinking: "Baked beans and brown bread on Saturday night, and news of Boston again. Soon I'll be at the Woodlawns'!"

Still another traveler had been on his way for months now. He had no steamboat tickets; he could not ask nor understand directions. He only knew that his nose and his heart were keeping him headed in the right direction. He was footsore and muddy and full of burrs. Sometimes he was hungry and heartsick and filled with despair, but he knew that he must get home. Sometimes he begged rides on boats similar to the boat which had carried him away. Sometimes people fed him, and he licked their hands, but he would never stay. Sometimes he caught rabbits or game birds for his food, and trotted through a tangled wilderness, lying at night beneath the stars to lick his weary feet and sleep. One day he trotted into the farmyard—so thin, so dirty, so footsore, and covered with burrs!

But Caddie Woodlawn knew him.·

"Nero!" she cried. "Nero! *Our own dog!*" and she sat right down where she was and took him in her arms and rocked him back and forth, her bright head pressed against the dog's rough coat. Nero yelped with joy and cried and licked her hands. Everybody ran out to see them, and it was the eighth wonder of the world that Nero had come home. They fed and washed and combed him, and in a week or so he looked very much like the dog which Uncle Edmund had taken away with him so long ago. To the end of his days Nero was a sheepdog, for never again did anyone try to educate him.

When the circuit rider came again, Caddie saw him far down the road as she had seen him in the spring, and she and Nero went to meet him. They stood at the gate and waited for him to come up, and a great many things went quickly through Caddie's mind.

"What a lot has happened since last year when I dropped the nuts all over the dining-room floor. How far I've come! I'm the same girl and yet not the same. I wonder if it's always like that? Folks keep growing from one person into another all their lives, and life is just a lot of everyday adventures. Well, whatever life is, I like it."

The late afternoon sun flooded her face with golden light. Looking toward the approaching rider, her face was turned to the west. It was always to be turned westward now, for Caddie Woodlawn was a pioneer and an American.

Caddie Woodlawn
By Carol Ryrie Brink

Reader's Guide

About the Book

Caddie Woodlawn is a real adventurer. She'd rather hunt than sew and plow than bake, and tries to beat her brother's dares every chance she gets. Caddie is friends with Indians, who scare most of her neighbors—neighbors who, like her mother and sisters, don't understand her at all.

Caddie is brave, and her story is special because it's true, based on the life and memories of Carol Ryrie Brink's grandmother, the real Caddie Woodlawn.

Discussion Topics

1. Describe Caddie Woodlawn. What kind of person is she? Give examples from the story that illustrate her personality.

2. In chapter one, the author writes that Caddie "was the despair of her mother and of her elder sister Clara." What does this mean? What is the reason for this? What were the roles of men, women, boys, and girls in early American society? How were children raised? How are the expectations of men, women, boys, and girls the same or different today?

3. Why did the Woodlawn family move from Boston to Wisconsin? What hardships did they and other pioneers face on their westward migration? Describe frontier life. How does the family adapt to life on the prairie? Compare it to the life they left behind.

4. Compare Caddie and Cousin Annabelle. In what ways are they the same? How are they different? What life lessons do the girls learn from each other?

5. What is the relationship between white settlers and Native Americans on the frontier? How do the two groups interact with each other? What stereotypes

and prejudices exist? How are friendships and alliances formed? Support your answers with examples from the text.

6. Describe the frontier school system. Where do the Woodlawn children go to school? In what ways is their school different from your school? What are the advantages and disadvantages of the frontier school?

7. How would life be different for the Woodlawn family if they had decided to move to England? List the pros and cons of making the move. Why did the family ultimately decide to stay in the U.S.? What would you have done if you were presented with a similar situation?

8. In the book's final chapter Caddie remarks upon the changes of the past year. "How far I've come!" she says. "I'm the same girl and yet not the same." Explain what Caddie means. What experiences have contributed to her self-development?

9. *Caddie Woodlawn* is a work of historical fiction. What does this mean? How is the genre the same as or different from other fiction? How does it compare to nonfiction? In her author's note, Carol Ryrie Brink writes that *Caddie Woodlawn* is based on real events, but that she has added to it "a few imaginary incidences." Select an incident that you believe to be imaginary and explain how it enhances the plot.

10. Carol Ryrie Brink was awarded the 1936 Newbery Medal for *Caddie Woodlawn*. Since 1922, the Newbery Medal has been presented to the author of the year's outstanding achievement in children's literature. What do you think makes the book a winner? Why do you think the book remains popular today?

Research & Activities
1. Research the historical time period in which *Caddie Woodlawn* is set. Think about what was happening in the U.S. at this time. Who was president? How many states were in the Union? What were the important issues of the period?

2. Write a series of diary entries from the perspective of one of the book's main characters. In your entries, incorporate information about the character's daily life and his or her hopes, dreams, and struggles, as well as his or her response to a particular event or situation that takes place in the book.

3. Read a map. Trace the Woodlawn family's route from Boston, Massachusetts, to western Wisconsin. What cities and states did they pass through on their journey? Were there any mountain ranges or rivers they had to cross? If so, what were they? On a Wisconsin state map, locate the places mentioned in the book, including the Menomonie (Red Cedar) River, Dunnville, Eau Galle, and Durand, Wisconsin.

4. Create a diorama to show the setting in which *Caddie Woodlawn* takes place. In your diorama, pay close attention to the natural and built environment. This includes the plants and animals found in the area, as well as human-made structures such as homes and schools.

5. Design a book jacket for *Caddie Woodlawn*. Choose a cover image that will attract readers and give them a hint as to what the story is about. On the front and back flaps, include a summary of the book and information about the author. You can also highlight short quotes about the book from class-mates who have read and enjoyed the book.

6. Make a glossary of new and different vocabulary words in *Caddie Woodlawn*. Include the word, its pronunciation, its part of speech, and a definition. Select words to illustrate.

7. Illustrate *Caddie Woodlawn*. Draw or paint pictures of the book's main characters and important scenes. Write a description to display alongside each of the images.

8. Design a poster meant to encourage westward migration. Think about what images or information might attract easterners to life on the western frontier.

Search the Internet and visit your local library or bookstore to get ideas for your poster.

9. Write a book review to convince others to read *Caddie Woodlawn*. Before you begin, read book reviews online or in the newspaper to get a feel for the kind of information to include, such as a general plot summary, your opinion about the book, and highlights from the book. With help from an adult, you may wish to post your review online at a bookseller's website.

10. Learn more about the oral tradition. As Carol Ryrie Brink explains in her author's note, *Caddie Woodlawn* is based on stories told to her by her grandmother. What stories have been passed down in your family? If you can't think of any, ask an adult family member to share with you a story from his or her childhood. Compose your own short story based on this information.

About the Author
Born in Moscow, Idaho, in 1895, Carol Ryrie Brink grew up hearing her grandmother's stories of frontier life in rural Wisconsin. She is the author of many books for young readers, including *Baby Island* and *Caddie Woodlawn's Family*.